# THE BOOK OF LAUGHTER

This is a collection of jokes edited by Ben Gonzales.

Side Splitting Hilarity!

Book of Laughs!

The best thing in life is laughter.

Jokes to share with everyone.

A laugh a day keeps the doctor away!

iUniverse, Inc.

New York   Bloomington

The Book of Laughs
jokes and short stories

This is a work of fiction. All of the characters, names, incidents,
organizations, and dialogue in this novel are either the products
of the author's imagination or are used fictitiously.

iUniverse books may be ordered through booksellers or by contacting:

iUniverse
1663 Liberty Drive
Bloomington, IN 47403
www.iuniverse.com
1-800-Authors (1-800-288-4677)

ISBN: 978-1-4401-2438-9 (pbk)
ISBN: 978-1-4401-2731-1 (ebk)

Printed in the United States of America

iUniverse rev. date: 10/6/2009

This book is dedicated to all my family and friends who shared their jokes with me and to all those who like a good joke. I began collecting jokes from friends and family 12 years ago and put them all together in this book to share with everyone.

Jacques Chirac, The French President, is sitting in his office when his telephone rings. "Hallo, Mr. Chirac!" a heavily accented voice said. "This is Paddy down at the Harp Pub in County Clare, Ireland. I am ringin to inform you that we are officially declaring war on you!"

"Well, Paddy," Chirac replied, "This is indeed important news! How big is your army?"

"Right now, " says Paddy, after a moments calculation, "there is meself, me Cousin Sean, me next door neighbor Seamus, and the entire darts team from the pub. That makes eight!"

Chirac paused. "I must tell you, Paddy, that I have 100,000 men in my army waiting to move on my command."

"Begoora!" says Paddy. "I'll have to ring you back."

Sure enough, the next day, Paddy calls again.

"Mr. Chirac, the war is still on. We have managed to get us som infantry equipment!"

"And what equipment would that be Paddy?" Chirac asks.

"Well, we have two combines, a bulldozer, and Murphy's farm tractor."

Chirac sighs, amused; "I must tell you, Paddy, that I have 6,000 tanks and 5,000 armored personnel carriers. Also, I have increased my army to 150,000 since we last spoke."

"Saints preserve us!" says Paddy. "I'll have to get back to yah."

Sure enough, Paddy rings again the next day.

"Mr. Chirac, the war is still on! We have managed to get ourselves airborne! We have modified Jackie McLaughlin's ultra-light with a couple of shotguns in the cockpit, and four boys from the Shamrock Bar have joined us as well!"

Chirac was silent for a minute then cleared his throat. "I must tell you, Paddy, that I have 100 bombers and 200 fighter planes. My military bases are surrounded by laser-guided, surface-to-air missile sites. And since we last spoke, I have increased my army to 200,000!"

"Jesus, Mary, and Joseph!" says Paddy, "I will have to ring you back."

Sure enough, Paddy calls again the next day.

"Top o' the mornin', Mr. Chirac! I am sorry to inform you that we have had to call off the war."

"Really, I am sorry to hear that," says Chirac. "Why the sudden change of heart?"

"Well, says Paddy, "we had a long chat over a few pints of Guinness, and decided there is no fookin' way we can feed 200,000 FRENCH prisoners."

### Smart Ass Answer of the Year:

A college teacher reminds her class of tomorrow's final exam. "Now class, I won't tolerate any excuses for you not being here tomorrow. I might consider a nuclear attack or a serious personal injury or illness, or a death in your immediate family, but that's it, no other excuses whatsoever!"
A smart ass guy in the back of the room raised his hand and asked, "What would you say if tomorrow I said I was suffering from complete and utter sexual exhaustion?" The entire class is reduced to laughter and snickering. When silence was restored, the teacher smiled knowingly at the student, shaking her head and sweetly said, "Well, I guess you'd have to write the exam with your other hand."

### Smart Ass Answer #2:

A truck driver was driving along on the freeway. A sign comes up that reads, "Low Bridge Ahead." Before he knows it, the bridge is right ahead of him and he gets stuck under the bridge. Cars are backed up for miles. Finally, a police car comes up. The cop gets out of his car and walks to the truck driver, puts his hands on his hips and says, "Got stuck, huh?" The truck driver says, "No, I was delivering this bridge and ran out of gas."

### Smart Ass Answer #3:

The cop got out of his car and the kid who was stopped for speeding rolled down his window. "I've been waiting for you all day," the cop said. The kid replied, "Yeah, well I got here as fast as I could." When the cop finally stopped laughing, he sent the kid on his way without a ticket.

Smart Ass Answer #4:

A lady was picking through the frozen turkeys at the grocery store, but she couldn't find one big enough for her family. She asked a stock boy, "Do these turkeys get any bigger?" The stock boy replied, "No ma'am, they're dead."

Smart Ass Answer #5:

A flight attendant was stationed at the departure gate to check tickets. As a man approached, she extended her hand for the ticket and he opened his trench coat and flashed at her. Without missing a beat…she said, "Sir, I need to see your ticket, not your stub."

My wife and I had words, but I didn't get to use mine.

As my five year old son and I were headed to McDonald's one day, we passed a car accident. Usually when we see something terrible like that, we say a prayer for those who might be hurt, so I pointed and said to my son, "We should pray." From the back seat I heard his earnest request: "Please, God, don't let those cars block the entrance to McDonald's."

Frustration is trying to find your glasses without your glasses.

Blessed are those who can give without remembering and take without forgetting.

The irony of life is that by the time you're old enough to know your way around, you're not going anywhere.

God made man before woman so as to give him time to think of an answer for her first question.

I was always taught to respect my elders, but it keeps getting harder to find one.

Every morning is the dawn of a new error.

I dialed a number and got the following recording: "I am not available right now, but thank you for caring enough to call. I am making some changes in my life. Please leave a message after the beep. If I do not return your call, you are one of the changes."

At pilots training back in the Air Corps they taught us, "Always try to keep the number of landings you make equal to the number of take offs you make."

Little Tommy had been to a birthday party at a friend's house. Knowing his sweet tooth, Tommy's mother looked straight in to his eyes and said, "I hope you didn't ask for a second piece of cake."
"No, but I asked Mrs. Smith for the recipe so you could make some like it, and she gave me two more pieces without asking."

Aspire to inspire before you expire.

A priest and a rabbi were sitting next to each other on an airplane. After a while, the priest turned to the rabbi and asked, "Is it still a requirement of your faith that you not eat pork?"
The rabbi responded, "Yes, that is still one of our beliefs."
Then the priest asked, "Have you ever eaten pork?"
To which the rabbi replied, "Yes, on one occasion I did succumb to temptation and tasted a ham sandwich."
The priest nodded in understanding and went on with his reading.
A while later, the rabbi spoke up and asked the priest, "Father, is it still a requirement of your church that you remain celibate?"
The priest replied, "Yes, that is still very much a part of our faith."
The rabbi then asked him, "Father, have you ever fallen to the temptations of the flesh?"
The priest replied, "Yes, rabbi, on one occasion I was weak and broke

my faith."

The rabbi nodded understandingly and remained silent, thinking, for about five minutes.

Finally, the rabbi said, "Beat a ham sandwich, didn't it?"

She spent the first day packing her belongings into boxes, crates and suitcases.

On the second day, she had the movers come and collect her things.

On the third day, she sat down for the last time at their beautiful dining table by candle-light, put on some soft background music, and feasted on a pound of shrimp, a jar of caviar, and a bottle of spring-water.

When she had finished, she went into each and every room and deposited a few half-eaten shrimp shells dipped in caviar into the hollow of the curtain rods.

She then cleaned up the kitchen and left. When the husband returned with his new girlfriend, all was bliss for the first few days.

Then slowly, the house began to smell.

They tried everything; cleaning, mopping, and airing the place out.

Vents were checked for dead rodents and carpets were steam cleaned.

Air fresheners were hung everywhere. Exterminators were brought in to set off gas canisters, during which they had to move out for a few days and in the end they even paid to replace the expensive wool carpeting. Nothing worked.

People stopped coming over to visit.

Repairmen refused to work in the house.

The maid quit.

Finally, they could not take the stench any longer and decided to move.

A month later, even though they had cut their price in half, they could not find a buyer for their stinky house.

Word got out and eventually even the local realtors refused to return their calls.

Finally, they had to borrow a huge sum of money from the bank to purchase a new place.

The ex-wife called the man and asked how things were going.

He told her the saga of the rotting house. She listened politely and said that she missed her old home terribly and would be willing to reduce her divorce settlement in exchange for getting the house back.

Knowing his ex-wife had no idea how bad the smell was, he agreed on a price that was about 1/10<sup>th</sup> of what the house had been worth, but only if she were able to sign the papers that very day.

She agreed and within the hour his lawyers delivered the paperwork.

A week later the man and his girlfriend stood smiling as they watched the moving company pack everything to take to their new home…

And to spite the ex-wife, they even took the curtain rods!!!!!

I love a happy ending, don't you?

## A Good Walk Never Hurts…

The room was full of pregnant women with their partners. The Lamaze class was in full swing. The instructor was teaching women how to breathe properly and was telling the men how to give necessary assurance to their partners at this stage of the pregnancy.

She said, "Ladies, remember that exercise is GOOD for you. Walking is especially beneficial. It strengthens the pelvic muscles and will make delivery that much easier!"

She looked at the men in the room. "And gentlemen, remember, you're in this together. It wouldn't hurt you to go walking with your partner."

The room suddenly got very quiet as the men absorbed this information. Then a man at the back of the room slowly raised his hand. "Yes?" said the teacher.

"I was just wondering," the man said. "Is it all right if she carries a golf bag while we walk?"

## I Think You're the Father of One of My Kids…

A guy goes to the supermarket and notices an attractive woman waving at him. She says hello.

He's rather taken back because he can't place where he knows her from.

So he says, "Do you know me?"

To which she replies, "I think you're the father of one of my kids."

Now his mind travels back to the only time he has ever been unfaithful to his wife and says,

"My God, are you the stripper from my bachelor party that I made love to on the pool table with all my buddies watching while your partner whipped my butt with wet celery???"

She looks into his eyes and says calmly, "No, I'm your son's teacher."


For Sale By Owner:

Complete set of Encyclopedia Britannica, 45 volumes

Excellent condition

$1,000 or best offer

No longer needed, got married last month.

Wife knows everything.


## Get out of the car!

(This is supposedly a true account recorded in the Police Log of Sarasota, Florida.)

An elderly Florida lady did her shopping and, upon returning to her car, found four males in the act of leaving with her vehicle.

She dropped her shopping bags and drew her handgun, proceeding to scream at the top of her lungs, "I have a gun, and I know how to use it! Get out of the car!"

The four men didn't wait for a second threat. They got out and ran like mad.

The lady, somewhat shaken, then proceeded to load her shopping bags into the back of the car and got into the driver's seat. She was so shaken that she could not get her key into the ignition.

She tried and tried, and then she realized why. It was for the same reason she had wondered why there was a football, a Frisbee and two 12-packs of beer in the front seat.

A few minutes later, she found her own car parked four or five spaces farther down.

She loaded her bags into the car and drove to the police station to report her mistake.

The sergeant to whom she told the story couldn't stop laughing.

He pointed to the other end of the counter, where four pale men were reporting a car jacking by a mad, elderly woman described as white, less than five feet tall, glasses, curly white hair and carrying a large handgun.

No charges were filed.

Moral of the story?

If you're going to have a senior moment…make it memorable.

Why doesn't Tarzan have a beard?

Why does Superman stop bullets with his chest, but ducks when you throw a revolver at him?

Why do Kamikaze pilots wear helmets?

Whose idea was it to put an "S" in the word "lisp"?

If people evolved from apes, why are there still apes?

Why is it that no matter what color bubble bath you use the bubbles are always white?

Is there ever a day that mattresses are not on sale?

Why do people constantly return to the refrigerator with hopes that something new to eat will have materialized?

Why do people keep running over a string a dozen times with their vacuum cleaner, then reach down, pick it up, examine it, then put it down to give the vacuum one more chance?

Why is it that no plastic bag will open from the end on your first try?

How do those dead bugs get in to those enclosed light fixtures?

When we are in the supermarket and someone rams our ankle with a shopping cart then apologizes for doing so, why do we say, "It's all right?" Well, it isn't all right, so why don't we say, "That hurt, you stupid idiot?"

Why is it that whenever you attempt to catch something that's falling off the table you always manage to knock something else off?

In winter why do we try to keep the house as warm as it was in summer when we complained about the heat?

Sign over a Gynecologist's office:
"Dr. Jones, at your cervix."

In a Podiatrist's office:
"Time wounds all heels."

On a septic tank truck:
"Yesterday's Meals on Wheels."

On a plumber's truck:
"We repair what your husband fixed."

On another plumber's truck:
"Don't sleep with a drip. Call your plumber."

On a church's bill board:
"7 days without God makes one weak."

On an electrician's truck:
"Let us remove your shorts."

In a Non-smoking area:

"If we see smoke, we will assume you are on fire and take appropriate action."

On a maternity room door:
"Push. Push. Push."

At an optometrists office:
"If you don't see what you're looking for, you've come to the right place."

On a taxidermist's window:
"We really know our stuff."

On a fence:
"Salesmen welcome! Dog food is expensive!"

At a car dealership:
"The best way to get back on your feet- miss a car payment."

Outside a car exhaust store:
"No appointment necessary. We hear you coming."

In a vet's waiting room:
"Be back in 5 minutes. Sit! Stay!"

In a restaurant window:
"Don't stand there and be hungry; come on in and get fed up."

In the front yard of a funeral home:
"Drive carefully. We'll wait."

And don't forget the sign at a radiator shop:
"Best place in town to take a leak."

<u>Four lessons to make you think about the way we treat people.</u>

1.) First important lesson- Cleaning Lady.

During my second month of college, our professor gave us a pop quiz. I was a conscientious student and had breezed through the questions until I read the last one: "What is the first name of the woman who cleans the school?" Surely this was some kind of joke. I had seen the cleaning woman several times. She was tall, dark-haired and in her 50's but how would I know her name?

I handed in my paper, leaving the last question blank. Just before class ended, one student asked if the last question would count toward our quiz grade. "Aboslutely," said the professor. "In your careers, you will meet many people. All are significant. They deserve your attention and care, even if all you do is smile and say "hello." I've never forgotten that lesson. I also learned her name was Dorothy.

2.) Second important lesson- Pickup in the Rain.

One night, at 11:30 p.m. an older African-American woman was standing on the side of an Alabama highway trying to endure a lashing rainstorm. Her car had broken down and she desperately needed a ride. Soaking wet, she decided to flag down the next car. A young white man stopped to help her, generally unheard of in those conflict-filled 60's. The man took her to safety, helped her get assistance and put her into a taxicab. She seemed to be in a big hurry, but wrote down his address and thanked him. Seven days went by and a knock came on the man's door. To his surprise, a giant color TV was delivered to his home. A special note was attached.

It read: "Thank you so much for assisting me on the highway the other night. The rain drenched not only my clothes, but also my spirits. Then you came along. Because of you, I was able to make it to my dying husband's bedside just before he passed away...God bless you for helping me and unselfishly serving others." Sincerely, Mrs. Nat King Cole

3.) Third important lesson- Always remember those who serve.

In the days when an ice cream sundae cost much less, a 10 year-old boy entered a hotel coffee shop and sat at a table. A waitress put a glass of water in front of him. "How much is an ice cream sundae?" he asked. "Fifty cents," replied the waitress. The little boy pulled his hand out of his pocket and studied the coins in it. "Well, how much is a plain dish of ice cream?" he inquired. By now more people were waiting for a table and the waitress was growing impatient. "Thirty-five cents," she brusquely replied. The little boy again counted his coins. "I'll have the plain ice cream," he said. The waitress brought the ice cream, put the bill on the table and walked away. The boy finished the ice cream, paid the cashier and left. When the waitress came back, she began to cry as she wiped down the table. There, placed neatly beside the empty dish, were two nickels and five pennies. You see, he couldn't have the sundae, because he had to have enough left to leave her a tip.

4.) Fourth important lesson- The obstacle in our path.

In ancient times, a King had a boulder placed on a roadway. Then he hid himself and watched to see if anyone would remove the huge rock. Some of the King's wealthiest merchants and courtiers came by and simply walked around it. Many loudly blamed the King for not keeping the roads clear, but none did anything about getting the stone out of the way.

Then a peasant came along carrying a load of vegetables. Upon approaching the boulder, the peasant laid down his burden and tried to move the stone to the side of the road. After much pushing and straining, he finally succeeded. After the peasant picked up his load of vegetables, he noticed a purse lying in the road where the boulder had been. The purse contained many gold coins and a note from the King indicating that the gold was for the person who removed the boulder from the roadway. The peasant learned what many of us never understand.

Some of the artists of the 60's are revising their hits with new lyrics to accommodate aging baby boomers. They include:

Bobby Darin-
Splish, Splash, I was havin' a Flash.
Herman's Hermits-
Mrs. Brown, You've got a lovely walker.
Ringo Starr-
I get by with a little help from my Depends.
The Bee Gees-
How can you mend a broken hip.

Roberta Flack-
The first time ever I forgot your face.
Johnny Nash-
I can't see clearly now.
Paul Simon-
Fifty ways to lose your liver.
The Commodores-
Once, Twice, Three times to the bathroom.
Marvin Gaye-
Heard it through the Grape Nuts.
Procol Harem-
A whiter shade of hair.
Leo Sayer-
You make me feel like napping.
The temptations-
Papa's got a kidney stone.
Abba-
Denture Queen.
Tony Orlando-
Knock 3 times on the ceiling if you hear me fall.
Helen Reddy-
I am woman, hear me snore.
Leslie Gore-
It's my procedure, and I'll cry if I want to.
Willie Nelson-
On the commode again.

Social Security Sex

Two men were talking. "So, how's your sex life?"
"Oh, nothing special. I'm having Social Security sex."
"Social Security sex?"
"Yeah, you know; I get a little each month, but not enough to live on!"

## Loud Sex

A wife went in to see a therapist and said, "I've got a big problem, doctor. Every time we're in bed and my husband climaxes, he lets out this ear splitting yell…"

"My dear," the shrink said, "that's completely natural. I don't see what the problem is."

"The problem is," she complained, "it wakes me up!"

## Quiet Sex

Tired of a listless sex life, the man came right out and asked his wife during a recent lovemaking session, "How come you never tell me when you have an orgasm?" She glanced at him and replied, "You're never home!"

## Confounded Sex

A man was in a terrible accident, and his "manhood" was mangled and torn from his body. His doctor assured him that modern medicine could give him back his manhood, but that his insurance wouldn't cover the surgery since it was considered cosmetic. The doctor said the cost would be $3,500 for "small", $6,500 for "medium," and $14,000 for "large." The man was sure he would want medium or large, but the doctor urged him to talk it over with his wife before he made any decision. The man called his wife on the phone and explained their options. The doctor came back into the room, and found the man looking dejected. "Well, what have the two of you decided?" asked the doctor. "She'd rather remodel the kitchen."

## Wedding Anniversary Sex

A husband and his wife had a bitter quarrel on the day of their 40th wedding anniversary. The husband yelled, "When you die, I'm getting you a headstone that reads: "Here lies my wife- Cold as ever"."

"Yeah," she replies, "when you die, I'm getting you a headstone that reads: "Here lies my husband- Stiff at last"."

## Women's Humorous Sex

My husband came home with a tube of KY Jelly and said, "This will make you happy tonight." He was right. When he went out of the bedroom, I squirted it all over the doorknobs. He couldn't get back in.

## Elderly Sex

One night, an 87 year-old woman came home from Bingo and found her 92 year-old husband in bed with another woman. She became violent and ended up pushing him off the balcony of their 20th floor, assisted living apartment, killing him instantly. Brought before the court on the charge of murder, the judge asked her if she had anything to say in her defense. She began coolly, "Yes, your honor. I figured that at 92, if he could have sex…he could also fly."

Actually, you can have a healthy sex life well into your later years. Assuming you can stand the sight of people your age naked.

## Intelligence Test

Here are 10 questions: You have 10 minutes only! DO NOT look at the answers found at the end of this page, that would be cheating! Remember, I am watching!

1.) Some months have 30 days, some months have 31 days. How many months have 28 days?

2.) If a doctor gives you 3 pills and tells you to take one pill every half hour, how long would it be before all the pills had been taken?

3.) I went to bed at eight o'clock in the evening and wound up my clock set the alarm to sound at nine o'clock in the morning. How many hours sleep would I get before being awaken by the alarm?

4.) Divide 30 by half and add ten. What do you get?

5.) A farmer had 17 sheep. All but 9 died. How many live sheep were left?

6.) If you had only one match and entered a COLD and DARK room, where there was an oil heater, an oil lamp and a candle, which would you light first?

7.) A man builds a house with four sides of rectangular construction, each side having a southern exposure. A big bear comes along. What color is the bear?

8.) Take 2 apples from 3 apples. What do you have?

9.) How many animals of each species did Moses take with him in the Ark?

10.) If you drove a bus with 43 people on board from Chicago and stopped at Pittsburgh to pick up 7 more people and drop off 5 passengers and at Cleveland to drop off 8 passengers and pick up 4 more and eventually arrive at Philadelphia 20 hours later, what's the name of the driver?

Answers

1.) All of them. Every month has at least 28 days.

2.) 1 hour: If you take a pill at 1 o'clock, then another at 1:30 and the last at 2 o'clock= 3 pills in 1 hour.

3.) 1 hour. It is a wind up alarm clock, cannot discriminate a.m. from p.m.

4.) 70. Dividing by half is the same as multiplying by 2.

5.) 9 live sheep.

6.) The match!

7.) White. If all walls face south, the house must be on the North Pole.

8.) 2 apples.

9.) None. It was Noah, not Moses.

10.) YOU are the driver!

Grading Scale (out of 10)
10 Genius
9 Mensa Member
8 Nuclear Engineer
7 High school pupil
6 College student
5 Porn Star
4 Used car salesman
3 Teacher

2 Doctor
1 University lecturer
0 Member of Congress

Back in cowboy times, a westbound wagon train was lost and low on food. No other humans had been seen for days, and then the pioneers saw an old Jew standing beneath a tree. "Is there some place ahead where we can get food?"

"Vell, I tink so," the old man said, "but I wouldn't go up dat hill und down de udder side. Somevun tole me you'd run into a big bacon tree."
"A bacon tree?" asked the wagon train leader. "Yah, a bacon tree. Vould I lie? Trust me. I vouldn't go dere." The leader goes back and tells his people what the old Jew said. "So why did he say not to go there?" a person asked. Other pioneers said, "Oh, you know those Jews- they have a thing about pork." So the wagon train goes up the hill and down the other side. Suddenly, Indians attack them from everywhere and massacre all except the leader who manages to escape and get back to the old Jew. Near dead, the man shouts, "You fool! You sent us to our deaths! We followed your route, but there was no bacon tree, just hundreds of Indians who killed everyone but me." The old man holds up his hands and says, "Vait a minute." He quickly picks up an English-Yiddish dictionary and begins thumbing through it. "Oy, I made such ah big mishtake! It vuzn't a bacon tree... (Are you ready?) You'll love this! "It vuz a ham bush."

This happened in a little town in New Mexico, and even though it sounds like an Alfred Hitchcock tale, it's absolutely true:
This guy was on the side of the road hitch hiking on a very dark and stormy night. The night was cold and wet and no cars went by. The storm was so strong he could hardly see a few feet ahead of him. Suddenly, he saw a car coming towards him and stopped. The guy, without thinking about it, got in the car, closed the door, and only then realized that there was nobody behind the wheel! The car starts going again, very slowly. The guy looks at the road and sees a curve

coming his way. Scared, he starts to pray and begs for his life. Just before the car hits the curve, a hand appears through the driver's window and turns the wheel. The guy, paralyzed in terror, watched how the hand appeared each time the car approached a curve. Gathering his strength, he gets out of the car and runs all the way to the nearest town. Wet and in shock, he goes into a cantina, asks for two shots of tequila and starts telling everybody about the horrible experience he just went through. A silence enveloped everyone when they realized the guy was crying hysterically and wasn't drunk. About a half hour later, two other guys walk into the same cantina and one said to the other, "Mira, vato. That's the Pendejo that got in the car while we were pushing it!"

## Golfer at the Dentist

A man and his wife walked into a dentist's office. The man said to the dentist, "Doc, I'm in one hell of a hurry. I have two buddies sitting out in my car waiting for us to go play golf, so forget about the anesthetic, just pull the tooth, and be done with it. We have a 10:00 a.m. tee time at the best golf course in town and it's 9:30 already. I don't have time to wait for the anesthetic to work!" The dentist thought to himself, "My goodness, this is surely a very brave man asking to have his tooth pulled without using anything to kill the pain." So the dentist asks him, "which tooth is it sir?" The man turned to his wife and said, "Open your mouth Honey, and show him."

## Doctors' Opinion of Financial Bail Out Package

The Allergists voted to scratch it, and the Dermatologists advised not to make any rash moves. The Gastroenterologists had sort of a gut feeling about it, but the Neurologists thought the Administration had a lot of nerve, and the Obstetricians felt they were all laboring under a misconception. The Ophthalmologists considered the idea shortsighted; the Pathologists yelled, "Over my dead body!" while the Pediatricians said, "Oh, grow up!" The Psychiatrists thought the whole idea was madness, the Radiologists could see right through it, and the Surgeons decided to wash their hands of the whole thing. The Internists thought it was a bitter pill to swallow, and the Plastic Surgeons said, "This puts a whole new face on the matter." The Podiatrists thought it was a step forward, but the Urologists felt the scheme wouldn't hold water. The Anesthesiologists thought the whole idea was a gas, and the Cardiologists didn't have the heart to say no. In the end, the Proctologists left the decision up to some assholes in Washington.

## Praise the Lord…

During the service, the pastor asked if anyone in the congregation would like to express praise for prayers which had been answered. A lady stood up and came forward. She said, "I have a reason to thank the Lord. Two months ago, my husband, Jim, had a terrible bicycle wreck and his scrotum was completely crushed. The pain was excruciating and the doctors didn't know if they could help him." You could hear an audible gasp from the men in the congregation as they imagined the pain that poor Jim experienced. She continued, "Jim was unable to hold me or the children and every move caused him terrible pain. We prayed as the doctors performed a delicate operation. They were able to piece together the crushed remnants of Jim's scrotum and wrap wire around it to hold it in place." Again, the men in the congregation squirmed uncomfortably as they imagined the horrible surgery performed on Jim. She continued, "Now, Jim is out of the hospital and the doctors say, with time, his scrotum should recover completely." All the men sighed with relief. The pastor rose and tentatively asked if anyone else has anything to say. A man rose and walked slowly to the podium. He said, "I'm Jim and I would like to tell my wife, the word is "sternum."

## Pants vs. Panties

Mike was going to be married to Karen so his father sat him down for a little chat. He said, "Mike, let me tell you something. On my wedding night in our honeymoon suite, I took off my pants, handed them to your mother, and said, "Here, try these on"." She did and said, "These are too big. I can't wear them." I replied, "Exactly. I wear the pants in this family and I always will." Ever since that night, we have never had any problems. "Hmmm," said Mike. He thought that might be a good thing to try. On his honeymoon, Mike took off his pants and said to Karen, "Here, try these on." She tried them on and said, "There are too large. They don't fit me." Mike said, "Exactly. I wear the pants in this family and I always will. I don't want you to ever forget that." Then Karen took off her panties and handed them to Mike. She said, "Here, you try on mine." He did and said, "I can't get into your panties.' Karen said, "Exactly. And if you don't change your smart-ass attitude, you never will."

Colored Panties

There were three old black ladies getting ready to take a plane across the ocean. The first lady said, "I don't know bout y'all, but I'm gunna wear me some hot pink panties beefo I gets on dat plane." Why you gonna wear dem fo?" the other two asked. The first replied, "Cause, if dat plane goes down and I'm out dare laying butt-up in a conefield, dey gonna find me first." The second lady said, "Well, I'm a-gonna wear me some flooresant orange panties."
"Why you gonna wear dem?" the others asked. The second lady answered, "Cause if dis hare plane is goin' down and I'm floating butt-up in the oshun, dey can see me first." The third old lady says, "Well, I'm not going to wear any panties…"
"What? No panties?" the others asked in disbelief. "Dat's right, you heard me. I'm not wearing any panties," the third lady said, "cause if dis plane goes down, honey, dey always look for da black box first!"

Why did the chicken cross the road?

Barack Obama: The chicken crossed the road because his coop was in foreclosure and it was time for change! The chicken wanted change!
John McCain: My friends, that chicken crossed the road because he recognized the need to engage in cooperation and dialogue with all the chickens on the other side of the road.
Hillary Clinton: I personally helped that little chicken to cross the road. Every chicken in this country deserves the chance to cross the road.

George W. Bush: We don't really care why the chicken crossed the road. We just want to know if the chicken is on our side of the road, or not. The chicken is either against us, or for us. There is no middle ground here.

Dick Cheney: Where's my gun?

Colin Powell: Now to the left of the screen, you can clearly see the satellite image of the chicken crossing the road.

Bill Clinton: I did not cross the road with that chicken. What is your definition of chicken?

Al Gore: I invented the chicken.

John Kerry: Although I voted to let the chicken cross the road, I am now against it! It was the wrong road to cross, and I was misled about the chicken's intentions. I am not for it now, and will remain against it.

Al Sharpton: Why are all the chickens white? We need some black chickens.

Dr. Phil: The problem we have here is that this chicken won't realize that he must first deal with the problem on this side of the road before it goes after the problem on the other side of the road. What we need to do is help him realize how stupid he's acting by not taking on his current problems before adding new problems.

Oprah: Well, I understand that the chicken is having problems, which is why he wants to cross this road so badly. So instead of having the chicken learn from his mistakes and take falls, which is a part of life, I'm going to give this chicken a car so that he can just drive across the road and not live his life like the rest of the chickens.

Anderson Cooper, CNN: We have reason to believe there is a chicken, but we have not yet been allowed to have access to the other side of the road.

Pat Buchanan: To steal the job of a decent, hardworking American.

Martha Stewart: No one called me to warn me which way that chicken was going. I had a standing order at the Farmer's Market to sell my eggs when the price dropped to a certain level. No little bird gave me any insider information.

Dr. Suess: Did the chicken cross the road? Did he cross it with a toad? Yes, the chicken crossed the road, but why it crossed I've not been told.

Ernest Hemingway: To die in the rain, alone.

Grandpa: In my day we didn't ask why the chicken crossed the road. Somebody told us the chicken crossed the road, and that was good enough.

Barbara Walters: Isn't that interesting? In a few moments, we will be listening to the chicken tell, for the first time, the heartwarming story of how it experienced a serious case of molting, and went on to accomplish its lifelong dream of crossing the road.

Aristotle: It is the nature of chickens to cross the road.

John Lennon: Imagine all the chickens in the world crossing the roads together, in peace.

Bill Gates: I have just released eChicken2008, which will not only cross roads, but will lay eggs, file your important documents, and balance your checkbook. Internet Explorer is an integral part of eChicken2008. This new platform is much more stable and will never reboot.

Albert Einstein: Did the chicken really cross the road, or did the road move beneath the chicken?

Colonel Sanders: Did I miss one?

Newspaper Headlines:

Federal Agents Raid Gun Shop, Find Weapons

One-armed man applauds the kindness of strangers

Alton attorney accidentally sues himself

County to pay $250,000 to advertise lack of funds

Volunteers search for old Civil War planes

Army vehicle disappears

Statistics show that teen pregnancy drops off significantly after age 25.

Utah Poison Control Center reminds everyone not to take poison.

Kids in Church

3 year-old Reese: "Our Father, Who does art in heaven, Harold is His name. Amen"

A little boy was overheard praying: "Lord, if you can't make me a better boy, don't worry about it. I'm having a real good time like I am."

After the christening of his baby brother in church, Jason sobbed all the way home in the back seat of the car. His father asked him three times what was wrong. Finally, the boy replied, "That preacher said he wanted us to be brought up in a Christian home, and I wanted to stay with you guys."

One particular 4 year-old prayed, "And forgive us our trash baskets as we forgive those who put trash in our baskets."

A Sunday school teacher asked her children as they were on the way to church service, "And why is it necessary to be quiet in church?" One bright little girl replied, "Because people are sleeping."

A mother was preparing pancakes for her sons, Kevin 5 and Ryan 3. The boys began to argue over who would get the first pancake. Their mother saw the opportunity for a moral lesson. "If Jesus were sitting her, He would say, "Let my brother have the first pancake, I can wait." Kevin turned to his younger brother and said, "Ryan, you be Jesus!"

A father was at the beach with his children when the 4 year-old son ran up to him, grabbed his hand and led him to the shore where a seagull lay dead in the sand. "Daddy, what happened to him?" the son asked. "He died and went to Heaven," the dad replied. The boy thought a moment and then said, "Did God throw him back down?"

A wife invited some people to dinner. At the table, she turned to their 6 year-old daughter and said, "Would you like to say the blessing?" "I wouldn't know what to say," the girl replied. "Just say what you hear Mommy say," the wife answered. The daughter bowed her head and said, "Lord, why on earth did I invite all these people to dinner?"

Believe it or not, these are Memphis, Tennessee real 911 calls!
Dispatcher: 911, what is your emergency?
Caller: I heard what sounded like gunshots coming from the brown house on the corner.
Dispatcher: Do you have an address?
Caller: No, I have on a blouse and slacks, why?

Dispatcher: 911, what is your emergency?
Caller: Someone broke into my house and took a bite out of my hand and cheese sandwich.
Dispatcher: Excuse me?
Caller: I made a ham and cheese sandwich and left it on the kitchen table and when I came back from the bathroom, someone had taken a bite out of it.
Dispatcher: Was anything else taken?
Caller: No, but this happened to me before and I'm sick and tired of it!

Dispatcher: 911, what is the nature of your emergency?
Caller: I'm trying to reach nine eleven but my phone doesn't have an eleven on it.
Dispatcher: This is nine eleven.
Caller: I thought you just said it was nine one one.
Dispatcher: Yes, ma'am nine one one and nine eleven are the same thing.
Caller: Honey, I may be old, but I'm not stupid.

Dispatcher: 911, what's the nature of your emergency?
Caller: My wife is pregnant and her contractions are only 2 minutes apart.

Dispatcher: Is this her first child?
Caller: No, you idiot! This is her husband!

Dispatcher: 911
Caller: Yeah, I'm having trouble breathing. I'm all out of breath. Darn, I think I'm going to pass out.
Dispatcher: Sir, where are you calling from?
Caller: I'm at a pay phone. North and Foster.
Dispatcher: Sir, an ambulance is on the way. Are you an asthmatic?
Caller: No.
Dispatcher: What were you doing before you started having trouble breathing?
Caller: Running from the police.

This is a non-partisan joke that can be enjoyed by both parties! Not only that- it is politically correct!
While walking down the street one day a US senator is tragically hit by a truck and dies. His soul arrives in heaven and is met by St. Peter at the entrance. "Welcome to heaven," says St. Peter. "Before you settle in, it seems there is a problem. We seldom see a high official around these parts, you see, so we're not sure what to do with you." "No problem, just let me in," says the man. "Well, I'd like to, but I have order from higher up. What we'll do is have you spend one day in hell and one day in heaven. Then you can choose where to spend eternity." "Really, I've made up my mind. I want to be in heaven," says the senator. "I'm sorry, but we have our rules." And with that, St. Peter escorts him to the elevator and he goes down, down, down to hell. The doors open and he finds himself in the middle of a green golf course. In the distance is a clubhouse and standing in front of it are all his friends and other politicians who had worked with him. Everyone is very happy and in evening dress. They run to greet him, shake his hand, and reminisce about the good times they had while getting rich at the expense of the people. They play a friendly game of golf and then dine on lobster, caviar and champagne. Also present is the devil, who really is a very friendly and nice guy who has a good time dancing and telling jokes. They are having such a

good time that before he realizes it, it is time to go. Everyone gives him a hearty farewell and waves while the elevator rises. The elevator goes up, up, up and the door reopens on heaven where St. Peter is waiting for him. "Now it's time to visit heaven." So, 24 hours pass with the senator joining a group of contented souls moving from cloud to cloud, playing the harp and singing. They have a good time and before he realizes it, the 24 hours have gone by and St. Peter returns. "Well, then, you've spent a day in hell and another in heaven. Now choose your eternity." The senator reflects for a minute, then he answers: "Well, I would never have said it before, I mean heaven has been delightful, but I think I would be better off in hell." So St. Peter escorts him to the elevator and he goes down, down, down to hell. Now the doors of the elevator open and he's in the middle of a barren land covered with waste and garbage. He sees all his friends, dressed in rags, picking up the trash and putting it in black bags as more trash falls from above. The devil comes over to him and puts his arm around his shoulder. "I don't understand," stammers the senator. "Yesterday I was here and there was a golf course and clubhouse, and we ate lobster and caviar, drank champagne, and danced and had a great time. Now there's just a wasteland full of garbage and my friends look miserable. What happened?" The devil looks at him, smiles and says, "Yesterday we were campaigning... Today you voted!"

## Italian Priests

Twelve Italian priests were about to be ordained. The final test was for them to line up in a straight row, totally nude, in a garden while a sexy, beautiful, big-breasted, nude model danced before them. Each priest had a small bell attached to his weenie, and they were told that anyone whose bell rang when she danced in front of them would not be ordained because he had not reached a state of spiritual purity. The beautiful model danced before the first candidate with no reaction. She proceeded down the line with the same responses from all the priests until she got to the final priest, Carlos. Poor Carlos. As she danced, his bell began to ring so loudly that it flew off, clattering across the ground and laid to rest in nearby foliage. Embarrassed,

Carlos quickly scrambled to where the bell came to rest. He bent over to pick it up and all the other bells started to ring!

These 16 police comments were taken off actual police car videos around the country.

16. "You know, stop lights don't come with any redder than the one you just went through."

15. "Relax, the handcuffs are tight because they're new. They'll stretch after you wear them a while."

14. "If you take your hands off the car, I'll make your birth certificate a worthless document."

13. "If you run, you'll only go to jail tired."

12. "Can you run faster than 1,200 feet per second? Because that's the speed of the bullet that'll be chasing you."

11. "You don't know how fast you were going? I guess that means I can write anything I want to on the ticket, hug?"

10. "Yes, sir, you can talk to the shift supervisor, but I don't think it will help. Oh, did I mention that I'm the shift supervisor?"

9. "Warning! You want a warning? O.K, I'm warning you not to do that again or I'll give you another ticket."

8. "The answer to this last question will determine whether you are drunk or not...Was Mickey Mouse a cat or a dog?"

7. "Fair? You want me to be fair? Listen, fair is a place where you go to ride on rides, eat cotton candy and corn dogs and step in monkey poop."

6. "Yeah, we have a quota. Two more tickets and my wife gets a toaster oven."

5. "In God we trust, all others we run through NCIC."

4. "How big were those 'two beers' you say you had?"

3. "No, sir, we don't have quotas anymore. We used to, but now we're allowed to write at many tickets as we can."

2. "I'm glad to hear that the Chief (of police) is a personal friend of yours. So you know someone who can post your bail."

1. "You didn't think we give pretty women tickets? You're right, we don't. Sign here."

These are actual comments made on students' report cards by teachers in the New York City public school system. All teachers were reprimanded.

1. Since my last report, your child has reached rock bottom and has started to dig.
2. I would not allow this student to breed.
3. Your child has delusions of adequacy.
4. Your son is depriving a village somewhere of an idiot.
5. Your son sets low personal standards and then consistently fails to achieve them.
6. The student has a "full six-pack" but lacks the plastic thing to hold it all together.
7. This child has been working with glue too much.
8. When your daughter's IQ reaches 50, she should sell.
9. The gates are down, the lights are flashing, but the train isn't coming.
10. If this student were any more stupid, he'd have to be watered twice a week.
11. It's impossible to believe the sperm that created this child beat out 1,000,000 others.
12. The wheel is turning but the hamster is definitely dead.


<u>Why we love children!!</u>

A kindergarten pupil told his teacher he'd found a cat, but it was dead. "How do you know that the cat was dead?" she asked him. "Because I pissed in its ear and it didn't move," answered the child innocently. "You did WHAT?!!" the teacher exclaimed in surprise. "You know," explained the boy, "I leaned over and went 'Pssst!' and it didn't move."

A little girl goes to the barber shop with her father. She stands next to the barber chair, while her dad gets his hair cut, eating a snack cake. The barber says to her, "Sweetheart, you're gonna get hair on your Twinkie." She says, "Yes, I know, and I'm gonna get boobs, too."

An exasperated mother, whose son was always getting into mischief, finally asked him, "How do you expect to get into Heaven?" The boy thought it over and said, "Well, I'll run in and out and in and out and keep slamming the door until St. Peter says, "For Heaven's sake, Dylan, come in or stay out!"

One summer evening during a violent thunderstorm a mother was tucking her son into bed. She was about to turn off the light when he asked with a tremor in his voice, "Mommy, will you sleep with me tonight?" The mother smiled and gave him a reassuring hug. "I can't dear," she said. "I have to sleep in Daddy's room." A long silence was broken at last by his shaky little voice: "The big sissy."

It was that time, during the Sunday morning service, for the children's sermon. All the children were invited to come forward. One little girl was wearing a particularly pretty dress and as she sat down, the pastor leaned over and said, "That is a very pretty dress. Is it your Easter Dress?" The little girl replied, directly into the pastor's clip on microphone, "Yes, and my mom says it's a b'tch to iron."

When I was six months pregnant with my third child, my three year-old came into the room as I was preparing to get into the shower. She said, "Mommy, you are getting fat!" I replied, "Yes, honey, remember mommy has a baby growing in her tummy." "I know," she replied, "but what's growing in your butt?"

One day the first grade teacher was reading the story of Chicken Little to her class. She came to the part where Chicken Little warns the farmer. She read, "...and Chicken Little went up to the farmer and said, "The sky is falling!" The teacher then asked the class, "And what do you think that farmer said?" One little girl raised her hand and said, "I think he said: "Holy Sh*t! A talking chicken!" The teacher was unable to teach for the next 10 minutes.

In the 1400's a law was set forth in England that a man was allowed to beat his wife with a stick no thicker than his thumb. Hence we have "the rule of thumb".

Many years ago in Scotland, a new game was invented. It was ruled "Gentlemen Only…Ladies Forbidden"…and thus the word GOLF entered into the English language.

The first couple to be shown in bed together on prime time TV were Fred and Wilma Flintstone.

Every day more money is printed for Monopoly than the U.S. Treasury.

Men can read smaller print than women can; women can hear better.

Coca-Cola was originally green.

It is impossible to lick your elbow.

The state with the highest percentage of people who walk to work: Alaska.

The percentage of North America that is wilderness: 38%

The cost of raising a medium-sized dog to the age of eleven: $16,400

The average number of people airborne over the U.S. in any given hour: 61,000

Intelligent people have more zinc and copper in their hair.

The first novel ever written on a typewriter: Tom Sawyer.

The San Francisco Cable cars are the only mobile National Monuments.

Each king in a deck of playing cards represents a great king from history: Spades- King David, Hearts- Charlemagne, Clubs-Alexander, the Great, and Diamonds- Julius Caesar

$$111, 111, 111 \times 111, 111, 111 = 12, 345, 678, 987,654,321$$

If a statue in the park of a person on a horse has both front legs in the air, the person died in battle. If the horse has one front leg in the air the person died as a result of wounds received in battle. If the horse has all four legs on the ground, the person died of natural causes.

Only two people signed the Declaration of Independence on July 4th; John Hancock and Charles Thomson. Most of the rest signed on August 2, but the last signature wasn't added until 5 years later.

Q. Half of all Americans live within 50 miles of what?
A. Their birthplace
Q. Most boat owners name their boats. What is the most popular boat name requested?
A. Obsession
Q. If you were to spell out numbers, how far would you have to go until you would find the letter 'A'?
A. One-thousand
Q. What do bulletproof vests, fire escapes, windshield wipers, and laser printers all have in common?
A. All were invented by women.
Q. What is the only food that doesn't spoil?
A. Honey
Q. Which day are there more collect calls than any other day of the year?
A. Father's Day

In Shakespeare's time, mattresses were secured on bed frames by ropes. When you pulled on the ropes the mattress tightened, making the bed firmer to sleep on. Hence the phrase…"Goodnight, sleep tight."

It was the accepted practice in Babylon 4,000 years ago that for a month after the wedding, the bride's father would supply his son-in-law with all the mead he could drink. Mead is a honey beer and because their calendar was lunar based, this period was called the honey month, which we know today as the honeymoon.

In English pubs, ale is ordered by pints and quarts...so in old England, when customers got unruly, the bartender would yell at them "Mind your pints and quarts, and settle down." It's where we get the phrase "mind your P's and Q's".

Many years ago in England, pub frequenters had a whistle baked into the rim or handle of their ceramic cups. When they needed a refill, they used the whistle to get some service. "Wet your whistle" is the phrase inspired by this practice.

At least 75% of people who read this will try to lick their elbow.

Don't overlook this just because it looks weird. Believe it or not, you can read it:
I cdnuolt blveiee taht I cluod aulaclty uesdnatnrd waht I was rdanieg. The phaonmneal pweor of the hmuan mnid aoccdrnig to rscheearch at Cmabrigde Uinervtisy, it deosn't mttaer in waht oredr the ltteers in a wrod are, the olny iprmoatnt tihng is taht the frist and lsat ltteer be in the rghit pclae. The rset can be a taotl mses and you can sitll raed it wouthit a porbelm. Tihs is bcuseae the huamn mnid deos not raed ervey lteter by istlef, but the wrod as a wlohe.

You know you are living in 2008 when...
1. You accidentally enter your PIN on the microwave.
2. You haven't played solitaire with real cards in years.
3. You have a list of 15 phone numbers to reach your family of three.
4. You e-mail the person who works at the desk next to you.
5. Your reason for not staying in touch with friends and family is that they don't have e-mail addresses.

6. You pull up in your own driveway and use your cell phone to see if anyone is home to help you carry in the groceries.

7. Every commercial on TV has a website at the bottom of the screen.

8. Leaving the house without your cell phone, which you didn't even have the first 20 or 30 (or 60) years of your life, is now a cause for panic and you turn around to go and get it.

10. You get up in the morning and go online before getting your coffee.

11. You start tilting your head sideways to smile. :)

12. You're reading this and nodding and laughing.

13. Even worse, you know exactly to whom you are going to send this message.

14. You are too busy to notice there was no #9 on this list.

15. You actually looked back to check that there wasn't a #9 on this list.

A little boy was attending his first wedding. After the service, his cousin asked him, "How many women can marry a man?" "Sixteen," the boy responded. His cousin was amazed that he had an answer so quickly. "How do you know that?" "Easy," the little boy said. "All you have to do is add it up, like the pastor said, 4 better, 4 worse, 4 richer, 4 poorer."

After church service on Sunday morning, a young boy suddenly announced to his mother, "Mom, I've decided to become a minister when I grow up." "That's okay with us, but what made you decide that?" "Well," said the little boy, "I have to go to church on Sunday anyway, and I figure it will be more fun to stand up and yell, than to sit and listen."

A 6 year-old was overheard reciting the Lord's Prayer at a church service, "And forgive us our trash passes, as we forgive those who passed trash against us."

A boy was watching his father, a pastor, write a sermon. "How do you know what to say?" he asked. "Why, God tells me." "Oh, then why do you keep crossing things out?"

A little girl became restless as the preacher's sermon dragged on and on. Finally, she leaned over to her mother and whispered, "Mommy, if we give him the money now, will he let us go?"

Ms. Terri asked her Sunday school class to draw pictures of their favorite Bible stories. She was puzzled by Kyle's picture, which showed four people on an airplane, so she asked him which story it was meant to represent. "The Flight to Egypt," was his reply. Pointing at each figure, Ms. Terri said, "That must be Mary, Joseph and Baby Jesus. But who's the fourth person?" "Oh, that's Pontius- the pilot!"

The Sunday school teachers asks, "Now, Johnny, tell me frankly do you say your prayers before eating?" "No sir," little Johnny replies, "I don't have to, my mom is a good cook."

A little girl was sitting on her grandfather's lap as he read her a bedtime story. From time to time, she would take her eyes off the book and reach up to touch his wrinkled cheek. She was alternately stroking her own cheek, then his again. Finally she spoke up, "Grandpa, did God make you?" "Yes, sweetheart," he answered, "God made me a long time ago." "Oh," she paused, "Grandpa, did God make me too?" "Yes, indeed, honey," he said, "God made you just a little while ago." Feeling their respective faces again, she observed, "God's getting better at it, isn't he?"

Farm Girl Birth Control

There were three gals who were getting married and all met at the marriage counselor's office to discuss the options of having or not having a baby right away. There were two city gals and one farm gal. The counselor asked them if they planned on having a baby right away or were going to wait awhile. They all agreed that they had discussed this with their potential husbands and all agreed to wait awhile. Well the counselor asked the first gal what type of birth control she planned to use. Her answer was the rhythm method. That will work, said the counselor if you keep a good record. He asked the second gal what system she planned on using. I plan on using birth control pills she said. Again, he said, yes that will work as long as you don't forget to take them. He then asked the farm girl what system she was planning on using. Her answer was The Pail and Saucer method. After a short delay, he again told her that should also work. He asked them all to come back in one year on a specific date for a follow up on how things were going. They all met again one year later and the two city gals were pregnant. Only the farm gal was slim and trim yet. Well the counselor asked the first gal what method she used and what went wrong. She replied that she used the rhythm method but somehow got her notes mixed up and, well here I am, going to have a baby. He asked the second city gal what method she used and she replied, the birth control pill but we were camping one weekend and I didn't have my pills with me and as you can see, I too am going to have a baby. He turns to the farm gal and told her that I vaguely remember you were going to use the pail and saucer method. Now, I must admit that I don't have a clue what the pail and saucer method is. Will you explain it to me as I see it had worked well for you. She replied, well we make love standing up, and since I am quite a bit taller than my husband, he stands on a pail turned upside down. Now, as we are making love, I watch his eyes and when his eyes get as big as saucers, I kick the pail out from under him!

## Irish Humor

Into a Belfast pub comes Paddy Murphy, looking like he'd just been run over by a train. His arm is in a sling, his nose is broken, his face is cut and bruised and he's walking with a limp. "What happened to you?" asks Sean, the bartender. "Jamie O'Conner and me had a fight," says Paddy. "That little shit, O'Conner," says Sean, "He couldn't do that to you, he must have had something in his hand." "That he did," says Paddy, "a shovel is what he had and a terrible lickin' he gave me with it." "Well," says Sean, "you should have defended yourself, didn't you have something in your hand?" "That I did," says Paddy.

"Mrs. O'Conner's breast and a thing of beauty it was, but useless in a fight."

An Irishman who had a little too much to drink is driving home from the city one night and of course his car is weaving violently all over the road. A cop pulls him over. "So," says the cop to the driver, "where have ya been?" "Why, I've been to the pub of course," slurs the drunk. "Well," says the cop, "it looks like you've had quite a few to drink this evening." "I did all right," the drunk says with a smile. "Did you know," says the cop, standing straight and folding his arms across his chest, "that a few intersections back, your wife fell out of your car?" "Oh, thank heavens," sighs the drunk. "For a minute there, I thought I'd gone deaf."

Brenda O'Malley is home making dinner, as usual, when Tim Finnegan arrives at her door. "Brenda, may I come in?" he asks. "I've somethin' to tell ya." "Of course you can come in, you're always welcome, Tim, but where's my husband?" "That's what I'm here to be telling ya, Brenda. There was an accident down at the Guinness brewery…" "Oh, God no!" cries Brenda. "Please don't tell me." "I must Brenda. Your husband Shamus is dead and gone. I'm sorry." Finally she looked up at Tim. "How did it happen, Tim?" "It was terrible, Brenda. He fell into a vat of Guinness Stout and drowned." "Oh my dear Jesus! But you must tell me true, Tim. Did he at least go quickly?" "Well, Brenda…no. In fact, he got out three times to pee."

Mary Clancy goes up to Father O'Grady after his Sunday morning service and she's in tears. He says, "So what's bothering you, Mary my dear?" She says, "Oh, Father, I've got terrible news. My husband passed away last night." The priest says, "Oh, Mary, that's terrible. Tell me, Mary, did he have any last requests?" She says, "That he did, Father." The priest says, "What did he ask, Mary?" She says, he said, "Please Mary, put down that damn gun…"

A drunk staggers into a Catholic Church, enters a confessional booth, sits down but says nothing. The Priest coughs a few times to get his attention but the drunk continues to sit there. Finally, the Priest pounds three times on the wall. The drunk mumbles, "Ain't no use knockin, there's no paper on this side either."

A guy goes to his doctor and says, "Doc, I have a problem. My girlfriend is sleeping over this Friday, my ex-wife is sleeping over this Saturday and my wife is coming home Sunday. I need 3 Viagra pills to satisfy them all." The doctor says, "You know, 3 Viagra pills taken 3 nights in a row is pretty dangerous for any man. I will give them to you on the condition that you return back to my office on Monday so that I can check you out." Monday morning the man returns with his right arm in a sling. The doctor asks, "What happened?" The man answered, "Nobody showed up!"

Miss Beatrice, the church organist, was in her eighties and had never been married. She was admired for her sweetness and kindness to all. One afternoon the pastor came to call on her and she showed him into her quaint sitting room. She invited him to have a seat while she prepared tea. As he sat facing her old pump organ, the young minister noticed a cut-glass bowl sitting on top of it. The bowl was filled with water. In the water floated, of all things, a condom! When she returned with tea and scones, they began to chat. The pastor tried to stifle his curiosity about the bowl of water and its strange floater, but soon it got to the better of him and he could no longer resist. "Miss Beatrice," he said, "I wonder if you would tell me about this?" pointing to the bowl. "Oh, yes" she replied, "Isn't it wonderful? I was walking through the park a few months ago and I found this little package on the ground. The directions said to place it on the organ, keep it wet and that it would prevent the spread of disease. Do you know I haven't had the flu all winter!" The pastor fainted.

### Grandma's Letter

The other day I went up to a local Christian bookstore and saw a "Honk if you love Jesus" bumper sticker. I was feeling particularly sassy that day because I had just come from a thrilling choir performance, followed by a thunderous prayer meeting, so I bought the sticker and put it on my bumper. I was stopped at a red light at a busy intersection, just lost in thought about the Lord and how good He is, and I didn't notice that the light had changed. It is a good thing someone else loves Jesus because if he hadn't honked, I'd never have noticed. I found that lots of people love Jesus. Why, while I was sitting there the guy behind me started honking like crazy, and when he leaned out of his window and screamed, "For the love of God, go go!" What an exuberant cheerleader he was for Jesus. Everyone started honking! I just leaned out of my window and started waving and smiling at all these loving people. I even honked my horn a few times to share in the love. There must have been a man from Florida back there because I heard him yelling something about a sunny beach. I saw another guy waving in a funny way with only his middle finger stuck up in the air. When I asked my teenage grandson in the back seat what that meant, he said that it was probably a Hawaiian good luck sign or something. Well, I've never met anyone from Hawaii, so I leaned out the window and gave him the good luck sign back. My grandson burst out laughing, why even he was enjoying this religious experience. A couple of the people were so caught up in the joy of the moment that they got out of their cars and started walking towards me. I bet they wanted to pray or ask what church I attended, but this is when I noticed that the light had changed. So, I waved to all my sisters and brothers, grinning, and drove on through the intersection. I noticed that I was the only car that got through the intersection before the light changed again and I felt kind of sad that I had to leave them after all the love we had shared, so I slowed the car down, leaned out of the window and gave them all the Hawaiian good luck sign one last time as I drove away.

No Sense of Humor

My wife and I are watching "Who Wants to be a Millionaire" while we are in bed. I turned to her and said, "Do you want to have sex?" "No," she answered. I then said, "Is that your final answer?" "Yes," she replied. Then I said, "I'd like to phone a friend." That's the last thing I remember.

A husband was in big trouble when he forgot his wedding anniversary. His wife told him, "Tomorrow there better be something in the driveway for me that goes zero to 200 in 2 seconds flat." The next morning the wife found a small package in the driveway. She opened it and found a brand new bathroom scale.

Funeral arrangements for the husband have been set for Saturday.

## SOMETHING TO OFFEND DAMN-NEAR EVERYBODY

1. What's the Cuban national anthem?

"Row, row , row your boat"

2. Where does an Irish family go on vacation?

A different bar

3. Did you hear about the Chinese couple that had a retarded baby? They named him "Sum Ting Wong"

4. What would you call it when an Italian has one arm shorter than the other?

A speech impediment

5. What does it mean when the flag at the Post Office is flying half-mast?

They're hiring.

6. Why aren't there any Puerto Ricans on Star Trek?

Because they're not going to work in the future either

7. What do you call an Arkansas farmer with a sheep under each arm?

A pimp

8. Why do drivers' education classes in Redneck schools use the car only on Mondays, Wednesdays and Fridays?

Because on Tuesday and Thursday the Sex Ed class uses it.

9. What's the difference between a southern zoo and a northern zoo?

A southern zoo has a description of the animal on the front of the cage, along with a recipe.

10. How do you get a sweet little 80 year-old lady to say the F word?

Get another sweet little 80 year-old to yell "BINGO!"

11. What's the difference between a northern fairytale and a southern fairytale?

A northern fairytale begins "Once upon a time…" A southern fairytale begins "Y'all ain't gonna believe this shit…"

12. My, my, how times have changed. Years ago…when 100 white men chased 1 black man we called it the Ku Klux Klan; Today they call it the PGA tour.

13. Why is there no Disneyland in China?

No one's tall enough to go on the good rides

## Moral of the Story

I was a very happy person. My wonderful girlfriend and I had been dating for over a year, and so we decided to get married. There was only one little thing bothering me…it was her beautiful younger sister. My prospective sister-in-law was twenty-two, wore very tight miniskirts, and generally was bra-less. She would regularly bend down when she was near me and I always got more than a pleasant view of her. It had to be deliberate. She never did it when she was near anyone else. One day her little sister called and asked me to come over to check the wedding invitations. She was alone when I arrived and she whispered to me that she had feelings and desires for me that she couldn't overcome. She told me that wanted to make love to me just once before I got married and committed my life to her sister. Well, I was in total shock and couldn't say a word. She said, "I'm going upstairs to my bedroom and if you want one last wild fling, just come up." I was stunned and frozen shock as I watched her go up the stairs. When she reached the top she blew me a kiss with a look that would make any man's heart beat faster. I stood there for a moment, then turned and made a beeline straight to the front door. I opened the door and headed straight towards my car. Lo and behold, my entire future family was standing outside, all clapping! With tears in his eyes, my father-in-law hugged me and said, "We are very happy that you have passed our little test. We couldn't ask for a better man for our daughter. Welcome to the family." And the moral of this story is: Always keep your condoms in your car!

Stumpy and his wife, Martha, went to the state fair every year. Every year Stumpy would say, "Martha, I'd like to ride in that there airplane." And every year Martha would say, "I know Stumpy, but that airplane ride costs ten dollars, and ten dollars is ten dollars." One year Stumpy and Martha went to the fair and Stumpy said, "Martha, I'm 71 years old. If I don't ride that airplane this year I may never get another chance." Martha replied, "Stumpy, that there airplane ride costs ten dollars, and ten dollars is ten dollars. The pilot overheard them and said, "Folks, I'll make you a deal. I'll take you both up for a ride if you can stay quiet for the entire ride and not say one word. I won't charge you, but if you say one word, it's ten dollars." Stumpy and Martha agreed and up they go. The pilot does all kinds of twists and turns, rolls and dives, but not one word is heard. He does all his tricks over again, but still not one word. They land and the pilot turns to Stumpy. "By golly, I did everything I could think of to get you to yell out, but you didn't." Stumpy replied, "Well, I was gonna say something when Martha fell out, but ten dollars is ten dollars."

Today I didn't do it!

One day, a man comes home from work to find total mayhem at home. The kids were outside, still in their pajamas, playing in the mud and muck. There were empty food boxes and wrappers all around. As he proceeded into the house, he found an even bigger mess. Dishes on the counter, dog food spilled on the floor, a broken glass under the table and a small pile of sand by the back door. The family room was strewn with toys and various items of clothing and a lamp had been knocked over. He headed up the stairs, stepping over the toys, to look for his wife. He was becoming worried that she may be ill or that something had happened to her. He found her in the bedroom, still in bed with her pajamas on, reading a book. She looked up at him, smiled, and asked how his day went. He looked at her bewildered and asked, "What happened here today?" She again smiled and answered, "You know every day when you come home from work and ask me what I did today?" "Yes," was his reply. She answered, "Well, today I didn't do it!"

<u>Can you figure these out?</u>

1. A murderer is condemned to death. He has to choose between three rooms. The first is full of raging fires, the second is full of assassins with loaded guns, and the third is full of lions that haven't eaten in 3 years. Which room is safest for him?
2. A woman shoots her husband. Then she holds him under water for over 5 minutes. Finally, she hangs him. But 5 minutes later they both go out together to enjoy a wonderful dinner together. How can this be?
3. What is black when you buy it, red when you use it, and gray when you throw it away?
4. Can you name three consecutive days of the week without using the words Monday, Tuesday, Wednesday, Thursday, Friday, Saturday, or Sunday?
5. This is an unusual paragraph. I'm curious how quickly you can find out what is so unusual about it. It looks so plain you would think nothing was wrong with it. In fact, nothing is wrong with it! It is unusual though. Study it, and think about it, but you still may not find anything odd. But if you work at it a bit, you might find out. Try to do so without any coaching!

Answers:
1. The third. Lions that haven't eaten in three years are all dead.
2. The woman was a photographer. She shot a picture of her husband, developed it and hung it up to dry.
3. Charcoal.
4. Sure you can: Yesterday, Today, and Tomorrow!
5. The letter "e," which is the most common letter in the English language does not appear once in the long paragraph.

Have you ever been guilty of looking at others your own age and thinking, "Surely I can't look that old?" Well, you'll love this one!
I was sitting in the waiting room for my first appointment with a new dentist. I noticed his DDS diploma, which bore his full name. Suddenly, I remembered a tall, handsome, dark-haired boy with the same name had been in my high school class some 40 odd years ago.

Could he be the same guy that I had a secret crush on way back then?? Upon seeing him, however, I quickly discarded any such thought. This balding, gray-haired man with a deeply lined face was way too old to have been my classmate. Hmm…or could he? After he examined my teeth, I asked him if he had attended Morgan Park High School. "Yes. Yes, I did. I'm a mustang," he gleamed with pride. "When did you graduate?" I asked. He answered, "In 1959. Why do you ask?" "You were in my class!" I exclaimed. He looked at me closely. Then that ugly, old, wrinkled, son-of-a-bitch asked, "What did you teach?"

## The Wash Cloth

I was due for an appointment with the gynecologist later in the week. But early on Monday morning, I received a call from his office to tell me that my appointment had been rescheduled for that morning at 9:30 am. I had just packed everyone off to work and school and it was already around 8:45 am. Since the trip to his office would take about 35 minutes, I didn't have any time to spare. As most women do, I like to take a little extra effort over hygiene when making such visits, but this time I wasn't going to be able to make the full effort. So, I rushed upstairs, threw off my pajamas, wet the washcloth that was sitting next to the sink, and gave myself a quick wash in "that area" to make sure I was at least presentable. I then threw the washcloth in the hamper, donned some clothes, hopped in the car and raced to my appointment. I was in the waiting room for only a few minutes when I was called in. Knowing the procedure, as I'm sure you do, I hopped up on the table, looked over at the other side of the room and pretended I was in Paris or some other place a million miles away. I was a little surprised when the doctor said, "My, we've made an extra effort this morning, haven't we?" I didn't respond. After the exam, I heaved a sigh of relief and went home. The rest of the day was normal…some shopping, cleaning, cooking, etc. After school, when my six year-old daughter was playing, she called out from the bathroom, "Mommy, where's my washcloth?" I told her to get another one from the cupboard. She replied, "No, I need the one that was here by the sink, it had all my glitter and sparkles saved inside it."

Jesse Jackson has a heart-attack and dies. He immediately goes to hell, where the devil is waiting for him. "I don't know what to do here," says the devil. "You are on my list, but I have no room for you. You definitely have to stay here, so I'll tell you what I'm going to do. I've got a couple of folks here who weren't quite as bad as you. I'll let one of them go, but you have to take their place. I'll even let you decide who leaves." Jesse thought that sounded pretty good, so the devil opened the door to the first room. In it, was Ted Kennedy, and a large pool of water. He kept diving in and surfacing, empty handed. Over and over and over he dove in and surfaced with nothing. Such was his fate in hell. "No," Jesse said. "I don't think so. I'm not a good swimmer and I don't think I could do that all day long." The devil led him to the door of the next room. In it was Al Gore with a sledgehammer and a room full of rocks. All he did was swing that hammer time after time after time. "No, I've got this problem with my shoulder. I would be in constant agony if all I could do was break rocks all day," commented Jesse. The devil opened a third door. Through it, Jesse saw Bill Clinton, lying on the floor with his arms tied over his head, and his legs restrained in a spread-eagle pose. Bent over him was Monica Lewinsky, doing what she does best. Jesse looked at this in shock and disbelief, and finally said, "Yeah, I can handle this." The devil smiled and said…"Ok, Monica, you're free to go."

## A Bad Day

An attorney got home late one evening, after a very taxing day trying to get a stay of execution for a client named Wright, who was due to be hanged for murder at midnight. His last minute plea for clemency to the governor had failed and he was feeling worn out and depressed. As soon as he got through the door at home, his wife started on him about, "What time of night do you call this? Where have you been?" and on and on. Too shattered to play his usual role in this familiar ritual, he went and poured himself a shot of whiskey and headed off for a long hot soak in the bathtub pursued by the predictable sarcastic remarks. While he was in the bath, the phone rang. The wife answered and was told that her husband's client had been granted his stay of execution after all. Finally realizing what a day he must have had, she decided to go upstairs to give him the good news. As she opened the bathroom door, she was greeted by the sight of her husband's rear end as he bent over naked drying his legs and feet. "They're not hanging Wright tonight," she said. He whirled around and screamed, "For crying out loud, woman, don't you ever stop!"

A man walks into a bar. He sees a good looking, smartly dressed woman perched on a bar stool. He walks up behind her and says, "Hi there good looking, how's it going?" She turns around, faces him, looks him straight in the eye and says, "Listen, I'll screw anybody, anytime, anywhere, your place, my place, it doesn't matter. I've been doing it ever since I got out of college. I just flat out love it." He says, "No kidding? I'm a lawyer too! What firm are you with?"

A guy sticks his head into a barber shop and asks, "How long before I can get a haircut?" The barber looks around the shop and says, "About 2 hours." The guy leaves. A few days later the same guy sticks his head in the door and asks, "How long before I can get a haircut?" The barber looks around at the shop full of customers and says, "About 3 hours." The guy leaves. A week later the same guy sticks his head in the shop and asks, "How long before I can get a haircut?" The barber looks around the shop and says, "About an hour and a half." The barber looks over at a friend in the shop and says, "Hey, Bill, follow that guy and see where he goes. He keeps asking how long he has to wait for a haircut, but then doesn't come back." A little while later, Bill comes back into the shop, laughing hysterically. The barber asks, "Bill, where does he go when he leaves here?" "Your house!"

Baseball and Nuts

A doctor at an insane asylum decided to take his patients to a baseball game. For weeks in advance, he coached his patients to respond to his commands. When the day of the game arrived, everything went quite well. As the National Anthem started, the doctor yelled, "Up Nuts," and the patients complied by standing up. After the anthem,

45

he yelled, "Down Nuts," and they all sat back down in their seats. After a home run was hit, the doctor yelled, "Cheer Nuts." They all broke out into applause and cheered. When the umpire made a particularly bad call against the star of the home team, the doctor yelled, "Booooo Nuts," and they all started booing and cat calling. Comfortable with their response, the doctor decided to get a beer and a hot dog, leaving his assistant in charge. When he returned, there was a riot in progress. Finding his frazzled assistant, the doctor asked, "What in the world happened?" The assistant replied, "Well, everything was going just fine until this idiot guy walked by and yelled, "Peanuts!"

## Jesus and the Redneck

An Irishman in a wheelchair entered a restaurant one afternoon and asked the waitress for a cup of coffee. The Irishman looked across the restaurant and asked, "Is that Jesus sitting over there?" The waitress nodded "yes," so the Irishman told her to give Jesus a cup of coffee on him. The next patron to come in was an Englishman with a hunched back. He shuffled over to a booth, painfully sat down, and asked the waitress for a cup of hot tea. He also glanced across the restaurant and asked, "Is that Jesus over there?" The waitress nodded, so the Englishman said to give Jesus a cup of hot tea, "My treat." The third patron to come into the restaurant was a Redneck on crutches. He hobbled over to a booth, sat down and hollered, "Hey there, sweet thang. How's about gettin' me a cold glass of Coke!" He, too, looked across the restaurant and asked, "Is that God's boy over there?" The waitress once more nodded, so the Redneck said to give Jesus a cold glass of Coke, "On my bill." As Jesus got up to leave, he passed by the Irishman, touched him and said, "For your kindness, you are healed." The Irishman felt the strength come back into his legs, got up, and danced a jig out the door. Jesus also passed by the Englishman, touched him and said, "For your kindness, you are healed." The Englishman felt his back straightening up, and he raised his hands, praised the Lord and did a series of back flips out the door. Then Jesus walked towards the Redneck. The Redneck jumped up and yelled, "Don't touch me...I'm drawin' disability."

## Missing Bill Clinton

Just watched a show on Canadian TV. There was a black comedian who said he misses Bill Clinton. "Yep, that's right- I miss Bill Clinton! He was the closest thing we ever got to having a black man as President."
Number 1- He played the sax.
Number 2- He smoked weed.
Number 3- He had his way with ugly white women.
Even now, look at him…his wife works, and he don't! And, he gets a check from the government every month.


Manufacturers announced today that they will be stocking America's shelves this week with "Clinton Soup," in honor of one of the nations' most distinguished me. It consists primarily of a weenie in hot water.
Chrysler Corporation is adding a new car to its line to honor Bill Clinton. The Dodge Drafter will be built in Canada.
When asked what he thought about foreign affairs, Clinton replied, "I don't know, I never had one."
American Indians nicknamed Bill Clinton "Walking Eagle" because he is so full of crap he can't fly.
Clinton lacked only three things to become one of America's finest leaders: integrity, vision and wisdom.
Clinton was doing the work of three men: Larry, Curly and Moe.
The Clinton revised judicial oath: "I solemnly swear to tell the truth as I know it, the whole truth as I believe it to be, and nothing but what I think you need to know."
Clinton will be recorded in history as the only President to do "Hanky Panky between Bushes".

## Little Johnny Strikes Again

Little Johnny watched his daddy's car pass by the school playground and go into the woods. Curious, he followed the car and saw Daddy and Aunt Jane in a passionate embrace. Little Johnny found this so exciting that he could not contain himself as he ran home and started to tell his mother, "Mommy, I was at the playground and I saw Daddy's car go into the woods with Aunt Jane. I went back to look and he was giving Aunt Jane a big kiss, then he helped her take off her shirt. Then Aunt Jane helped Daddy take his pants off, then Aunt Jane…" At this point Mommy cut him off and said, "Johnny, this is such an interesting story, suppose you save the rest of it for supper time. I want to see the look on Daddy's face when you tell it tonight."! At the dinner table Mommy asked Little Johnny to tell his story. Johnny started his story, "I was at the playground and I saw Daddy's car go into the woods with Aunt Jane. I went back to look and he was giving Aunt Jane a big kiss, then he helped her take off her shirt. Then Aunt Jane helped Daddy take his pants off, then Aunt Jane and Daddy started doing the same thing that Mommy and Uncle Bill used to do when Daddy was in the Army."

Moral: Sometimes you need to listen to the whole story before you interrupt.

Denver Airport: An award should go to United Airlines gate agent in Denver for being smart and funny, while making her point, when confronted with a passenger who probably deserved to fly as cargo. A crowded United Airlines flight was canceled. A single agent was re-booking a long line of inconvenienced travelers. Suddenly an angry passenger pushed his way to the desk. He slapped his ticket on the counter and said, "I have to be on this flight and it has to be FIRST CLASS." The agent replied, "I am sorry, sir. I'll be happy to try to help you, but I've got to help these folks first, and I'm sure we'll be able to work something out." The passenger was unimpressed. He asked loudly, so that the passengers behind him could hear, "Do you have any idea who I am?" Without hesitating, the agent smiled and grabbed her public address microphone. "May I have your attention please," she began, her voice heard clearly throughout the terminal. "We have a passenger here at Gate 14 who does not know who he is. If anyone can help him find his identity, please come to Gate 14." With the folks behind him in the line laughing hysterically, the man glared at the United agent, gritted his teeth and swore, "F*** You!". Without flinching, she smiled and said "I'm sorry sir, you'll have to get in line for that too."

## The Best Comeback Line Ever:

Marine Corp's General Reinwald was interviewed on the radio and you have to read his reply to the lady who interviewed him concerning guns and children.

This is a portion of a National Public Radio (NPR) interview between a female broadcaster and US Marine Corps General Reinwald who was about to sponsor a Boy Scout Troop visiting his military installation.

Female Interviewer: So, General Reinwald, what things are you going to teach these young boys when they visit your base?

General Reinwald: We're going to teach them climbing, canoeing, archery and shooting.

Female Interviewer: Shooting! That's a bit irresponsible, isn't it?

General Reinwald: I don't see why, they'll be properly supervised on the rifle range.

Female Interviewer: Don't you admit that this is a terribly dangerous activity to be teaching children?

General Reinwald: I don't see how. We will be teaching them proper rifle discipline before they even touch a firearm.

Female Interviewer: But you're equipping them to become violent killers.

General Reinwald: Well, Ma'am, you're equipped to be a prostitute, but you're not one, are you?

The radio went silent and the interview ended.

## Waking Up for Church

One Sunday morning, a mother went in to wake her son and tell him it was time to get ready for church, to which he replied, "I'm not going." "Why not?" she asked. "I'll give you two good reasons," he said. "One, they don't like me, and two, I don't like them." His mother replied, "I'll give YOU two good reason why YOU SHOULD go to church. "One, you're 59 years old, and two, you're the pastor!"

## The Picnic

A Jewish Rabbi and a Catholic Priest met at the town's annual 4th of July picnic. "Old friends," they began their usual banter, "This baked ham is really delicious," the priest teased the rabbi. "You really ought to try it. I know it's against your religion, but I can't understand why such a wonderful food should be forbidden! You don't know what you're missing. You haven't lived until you've tried Mrs. Hall's prized Virgin Baked Ham. Tell me, Rabbi, when are you going to break down and try it?" The rabbi looked at the priest with a big grin, and said, "At your wedding."

## The Usher

An elderly woman walked into the local country church. The friendly usher greeted her at the door and helped her up the flight of steps. "Where would you like to sit?" he asked politely. "The front row please," she answered. "You really don't want to do that," the usher said. "The pastor is really boring." "Do you happen to know who I am?" the woman inquired. "No," he said. "I'm the pastor's mother," she replied indignantly. "Do you know who I am?" he asked. "No," she said. "Good," he answered.

## Show and Tell

A kindergarten teacher gave her class a "Show and Tell" assignment. Each student was instructed to bring in an object to share with the class that represented their religion. The first student got up in front of the class and said, "My name is Benjamin and I am Jewish and this is a Star of David." The second student go up in front of the class and said, "My name is Mary. I'm a Catholic and this is a Rosary." The third student got up in front of the class and said, "My name is Tommy. I am Methodist, and this is a casserole."

## Over the Best Way to Pray

A priest, a minister and a guru sat discussing the best positions for prayer, while a telephone repairman worked nearby. "Kneeling is definitely the best way to pray," the priest said. "No," said the minister. "I get the best results standing with my hands outstretched to Heaven." "You're both wrong," the guru said. "The most effective prayer position is lying down on the floor." The repairman could contain himself no longer. "Hey fellas," he interrupted. "The best prayin' I ever did was when I was hangin' upside down from a telephone pole."

## The Twenty and the One

A well-worn one-dollar bill and a similarly distressed twenty-dollar bill arrived at the Federal Reserve Bank to be retired. As they moved along the conveyor belt to be burned, they struck up a conversation. The twenty-dollar bill reminisced about its travels all over the country. "I've had a pretty good life," the twenty proclaimed. "Why I've been to Las Vegas, Atlantic City, the finest restaurants in New York, performances on Broadway, and even a cruise to the Caribbean." "Wow!" said the one-dollar bill. "You've really had an exciting life!" "So tell me," says the twenty, "where have you been throughout your lifetime?" The one-dollar bill replies, "Oh, I've been to the Methodist Church, the Baptist Church, the Lutheran Church…" The twenty-dollar bill interrupts, "What's a church?"

## Goat for Dinner

The young couple invited their elderly pastor for Sunday dinner. While they were in the kitchen preparing the meal, the minister asked their son what they were having. "Goat," the little boy replied. "Goat?" replied the startled man of the cloth, "Are you sure about that?""Yep," said the youngster. "I heard Dad say to Mom, "Today is just as good as any to have the old goat for dinner."

## Wyoming Stories

#1 The owner of a golf course in Lusk was confused about paying an invoice, so he decided to ask his secretary for some mathematical help. He called her into his office and said, "You graduated from the University of Nebraska and I need some help. If I were to give you $20,000, minus 14%, how much would you take off?" The secretary thought a moment, then replied, "Everything but my earrings."

#2 A group of Nebraska friends, hunting in Wyoming went deer hunting and paired off in twos for the day. That night, one of the hunters returned alone, staggering under the weight of an eight-point buck. "Where's Henry?" the others asked. "Henry had a stroke of some kind. He's a couple of miles back up the trail," the successful hunter replied. "You left Harry laying out there and carried the deer back?" they inquired. "A tough call," nodded the hunter. "But I figured no one is going to steal Henry!"

An old hillbilly farmer had a wife who nagged him unmercifully. From morning till night (and sometimes later), she was always complaining about something. The only time he got any relief was when he was out plowing with his old mule. He tried to plow a lot. One day, when he was out plowing, his wife brought him lunch in the field. He drove the old mule into the shade, sat down on a stump, and began to eat his lunch. Immediately his wife began nagging him again. Complain, nag, nag; it just went on and on. All of a sudden, the old mule lashed out with both hind feet; caught her smack in the back of the head. Killed her dead on the spot. At the funeral several days later, the minister noticed something rather odd. When a woman mourner would approach the old farmer, he would listen for a minute, then nod his head in agreement; but when a man mourner approached him, he would listen for a minute, then shake his head in disagreement. This was so consistent, the minister decided to ask the old farmer about it. So after the funeral, the minister spoke to the old farmer, and asked him why he nodded his head and agreed with the woman, but always shook his head and disagreed with all the men. The old farmer said: "Well, the women would come up and say something about how nice my wife looked, or how pretty her dress was, so I'd nod my head in agreement." "And what about the men?" the minister asked. "They wanted to know if the mule was for sale."

## New York Cab Drivers

A woman and her son were taking a cab in New York City. It was raining and all the hookers were standing under the awnings. "Mom," said the little boy, "what are all those women doing?" "They're waiting for their husbands to get off work," she replied. The cabbie turns around and says, "Geez lady, why don't you tell him the truth? They're hookers, boy! They have sex with men for money." The little boys eyes get wide-eyed and he says, "Is that true, Mom?" His mother glaring hard at the cabbie, answers in the affirmative. After a few minutes, the kid asks, "Mom, what happens to the babies those women have?" "Most of them are cab drivers," she replied.

A girl came skipping home from school one day. "Mommy, Mommy," she yelled, "we were counting today and all the other kids could only count to four, but I counted to 10. See? 1, 2, 3, 4, 5, 6, 7, 8, 9, 10!" "Very good," said her mother. "Is it because I'm blonde?" the girl said. "Yes, it's because you're blonde," said the mommy. The next day the girl came skipping home from school. "Mommy, Mommy," she yelled, "we were saying the alphabet today and all the other kids could only say it to D, but I said to G. See? A, B, C, D, E, F, G!" "Very good," said her mother. "Is it because I'm blonde, Mommy?" "Yes, it's because you're blonde." The next day the girl came skipping home from school. "Mommy, Mommy," she yelled, "we were in gym class today and when we showered all the other girls had flat chests, but I have these!" And she lifted her tank top to reveal a pair of 36 C's. "Very good," said her embarrassed mother. "Is it because I'm blonde, mommy?" "No, honey, it's because you're 24."

## Tennessee

A guy from Tennessee passed away and left his entire estate to his beloved widow, but she can't touch it 'til she's 14.
How do you know when you're staying in a Tennessee hotel? When you call the front desk and say, "I gotta leak in my sink," and the clerk replies, "Go ahead."

How can you tell if a Tennessee redneck is married? There's dried tobacco juice on both sides of his pickup truck.

Did you hear that they have raised the minimum drinking age in Tennessee to 32? It seems they want to keep alcohol out of the high schools.

What do they call reruns of "Hee Haw" in Tennessee? Documentaries.

Where was the toothbrush invented? Tennessee. If it had been invented anywhere else, it would been called a teethbrush.

A Tennessee state trooper pulls over a pickup on I-64 and says to the driver, "Gotany I.D.?" and the driver replies, "Boutwut?"

Did you hear about the $3 million Tennessee state lottery? The winner gets $3.00 a year for a million years.

The Governor's mansion in Tennessee burned down! Yep. Pert' near took out the whole trailer park. The library was a total loss, too. Both books-POOF-up in flames and he hadn't even finished coloring one of them.

A new law was recently passed in Tennessee. When a couple gets divorced, they are STILL cousins.

A guy walks into a bar in Tennessee and orders a mudslide. The bartender looks at the man and says, "You ain't from 'round here are ya?" "No," replies the man, "I'm from Pennsylvania." The bartender looks at him and says, "Well, what do ya do in Pennsylvania?" "I'm a taxidermist," said the man. The bartender, looking very bewildered now, asks, "What in the world is a tax-e-derm-ist?" "The man says, "I mount animals". The bartender stands back and hollers to the whole bar... "It's okay boys, he's one of us!"

My son is under a doctor's care and should not take PE today, please execute him.

Please excuse Lisa for being absent she was sick and I had her shot.

Dear School: Please excuse John being absent on Jan. 28, 29, 30, 31, 32 and also 33.

Please excuse Gloria from Jim today. She is administrating.

Please excuse Roland from P.E. for a few days. Yesterday he fell out of a tree and misplaced his hip.

John has been absent because he had two teeth taken out of his face.

Carlos was absent yesterday because he was playing football. He was hurt in the growing part.

Megan could not come to school today because she has been bothered by very close veins.

Chris will not be school cus he has an acre in his side.

Please excuse Ray Friday from school. He has very loose vowels.

Please excuse Pedro from being absent yesterday. He had (diahre, dyrea, direathe), the shits. Words in ()'s were crossed out.

Please excuse Tommy for being absent yesterday. He had diarrhea, and his boots leak.

Irving was absent yesterday because he missed his bust.

Please excuse Jimmy for being. It was his father's fault.

I kept Billie home because she had to go Christmas shopping because I don't know what size she wears.

Please excuse Jennifer for missing school yesterday, we forgot to get the Sunday paper off the porch, and when we found it Monday, we thought it was Sunday.

Sally won't be in school a week from Friday. We have to attend her funeral.

My daughter was absent yesterday because she was tired. She spent a weekend with the Marines.

Please excuse Jason for being absent yesterday. He had a cold and could not breed well.

Please excuse Mary for being absent yesterday. She was in bed with Gramps.

Gloria was absent yesterday as she was having a gangover.

Please excuse Brenda. She has been sick and under the doctor.

Maryann was absent December 11-16, because she had a fever, sore throat, headache and upset stomach. Her sister was also sock, fever and sore throat. Her brother had a low grade fever and ached all over. I wasn't the best either, sore throat and fever. There must be something going around, her father even got hot last night.

## Some old, Some New, Some Good, Some ????

I was in the express lane at the store quietly fuming. Completely ignoring the sign, the woman ahead of me had slipped into the chick-out line pushing a cart piled high with groceries. Imagine my delight when the cashier beckoned the woman to come forward looked into the car and asked sweetly, "So which six items would you like to buy?"

Because they had no reservations at a busy restaurant, my elderly neighbor and his wife were told there would be a 45-minute wait for a table. "Young man, we're both 90 years old," the husband said. "We may not have 45 minutes." They were seated immediately.

The reason congressmen try so hard to get re-elected is that they would hate to have to make a living under the laws they've passed.

All eyes were on the radiant bride as her father escorted her down the aisle. They reached the altar and the waiting groom; the bride kissed her father and placed something in his hand. The guests in the front pews responded with ripples of laughter. Even the priest smiled broadly. As her father gave her away in marriage, the bride gave him back his credit card.

Woman and cats will do as they please, and men and dogs should relax and get used to the idea.

Three friends from the local congregation were asked "When you're in your casket, and friends and congregation members are mourning over you, what would you like them to say?" Artie said: "I would like them to say I was a wonderful husband, a fine spiritual leader, and a great family man." Eugene comment: I would like them to say I was a wonderful teacher and servant of God who made a huge difference in people's lives." Don said: I'd like them to say, "Look, he's moving!"

Smith climbs to the top of Mt. Sinai to get close enough to talk to God. Looking up, he asks the Lord, "God, what does a million years mean to you?" The Lord replies, "A minute." Smith asks, "And what does a million dollars mean to you?" The Lord replies, "A penny." Smith asks, "Can I have a penny?" The Lord replies, "In a minute."

A man goes to a shrink and says, "Doctor, my wife is unfaithful to me. Every evening, she goes to Larry's bar and picks up men. IN fact, she sleeps with anybody who asks her! I'm going crazy. What do you think I should do?" "Relax," says the Doctor, "take a deep breath and calm down. Now, tell me, exactly where is Larry's bar?"

An old man goes to the Wizard to ask him if he can remove a "Curse" he has been living with for the last 40 years. The Wizard says "Maybe, but you will have to tell me the exact words that were used to put the curse on you." The old man says without hesitation, "I now pronounce you man and wife."

John was on his deathbed and gasped pitifully. "Give me one last request, dear," he said. "Of course, John," his wife said softly. "Six months after I die," he said, "I want you to marry Bob." "But I thought you hated Bob," she said. With his last breath John said, "I do!"

A man picks up a young woman in a bar and convinces her to come back to his hotel. When they are relaxing afterwards, he asks, "Am I the first man you ever made love to?" She looks at him thoughtfully for a second before replaying. "You might be," she says. "Your face looks familiar."

A man goes to see the Rabbi. "Rabbi, something terrible is happening and I have to talk to you about it." The Rabbi asked, "What's wrong?" The man replied, "My wife is poisoning me." The Rabbi, very surprised by this, asks, "How can that be?" The man then pleads, "I'm telling you, I'm certain she's poisoning me, what should I do?" The Rabbi then offer, "Tell you what. Let me talk to her, I'll see what I can find out and I'll let you know." A week later the Rabbi calls the man and says, "Well, I spoke to your wife. I spoke to her on the phone for three hours. You want my advice?" The man said yes and the Rabbi replied, "Take the poison."

An atheist was taking a walk through the woods. What majestic trees! What powerful rivers! What beautiful animals!" he said to himself. As he was walking alongside the river he heard a rustling in the bushes behind him. He turned to look. He saw a 7 foot grizzly charge towards him. He ran as fast as he could up the path. He looked over his shoulder and saw that the bear was closing in on him. He looked over his shoulder again, and the bear was even closer. He tripped and fell on the ground. He rolled over to pick himself up but saw the bear right on top of him, reaching for him with his left paw and raising his right paw to strike him. At that instant the Atheist cried out: "Oh my god!..." Time stopped. The bear froze. The forest was silent. As a bright light shone upon the man, a voice came out of the sky: "You deny my existence for all of these years, teach others I don't exist, and even credit creation to a cosmic accident. Do you expect me to help you out of this predicament? Am I to count you as a believer?" The atheist looked directly into the light, "It would be hypocritical of me to suddenly ask You to treat me as a Christian now, but perhaps could you make the BEAR a Christian?" "Very well," said the voice. The light went out. The sounds of the forest resumed. And then the bear dropped his right paw, brought both paws together and bowed his head and spoke: "Lord, bless this food, which I am about to receive from thy bounty through Christ our Lord, Amen."

A tour bus driver drives with of bus full of seniors down a highway, when he is tapped on his shoulder by a little old lady. She offers him a handful of peanuts, which he gratefully munches up. After approx. 15 minutes, she taps him on his shoulder again and she hands him another handful of peanuts. She repeats this gesture about eight times. At the ninth time he asks the little old lady why they do not eat the peanuts themselves, whereupon she replies that it is not possible because of their old teeth, they are not able to chew them. "Why do you buy them then?" he asks puzzled. Whereupon the old lady answers, "We just love the chocolate around them."

Why you can't send a woman to the hardware store.
Bubba was fixing a door and he found that he needed a new hinge, so he sent his wife Mary Louise to the hardware store. At the hardware store Mary Louise saw a beautiful teapot on a top shelf while she was waiting for Joe Bob, the manager, to finish waiting on a customer. When Joe Bob was finished, Mary Louise asked how much for the teapot. Joe Bob replied, "That's silver and it costs $100!" "My goodness, that sure is a lotta money!" Mary Louise exclaimed. Then she proceeded to describe the hinge that Bubba had sent her to buy, and Joe Bob went to the back room to find it. From the back room Joe Bob yelled, "Mary Louise, you want screw for that hinge?" To which Mary Louise replied, "No, but I will for the teapot."

There was a very gracious lady who was mailing an old family Bible to her brother in another part of the country. "Is there anything breakable in here?" asked the postal clerk. "Only the Ten Commandments," answered the lady.

Somebody has said there are only two kinds of people in the world. There are those who wake up in the morning and say, "Good morning, Lord," and there are those who wake up in the morning and say, "Good Lord, it's morning."

A minister parked his car in a no-parking zone in a large city because he was short of time and couldn't find a space with a meter. Then he put a note under the windshield wiper that read: "I have circled the block 10 times. If I don't park here, I'll miss my appointment. Forgive us our trespasses." When he returned, he found a citation from a police officer along with this note "I've circle this block for 10 years. If I don't give you a ticket I'll lose my job. Lead us not into temptation."

There is the story of a pastor who got up one Sunday and announced to his congregation: "I have good news and bad news. The good news is, we have enough money to pay for our new building program. The bad news is, it's still out there in your pockets."

While driving in Pennsylvania, a family caught up to an Amish carriage. The owner of the carriage obviously had a sense of humor, because attached to the back of the carriage was a hand printed sign… "Energy efficient vehicle: Runs on oats and grass. Caution: Do not step in exhaust."

A Sunday school teacher began her lesson with a question, "Boys and girls, what do we know about God?" A hand shot up in the air. "He is an artist!" said the kindergarten boy. "Really? How do you know?" the teacher asked. "You know – Our Father, who does art in heaven…"

A minister waited in line to have his car filled with gas just before a long holiday weekend. The attendant worked quickly, but there were many cars ahead of him. Finally, the attendant motioned him toward a vacant pump. "Reverend," said the young man, "I'm so sorry about the delay. It seems as if everyone waits until the last minute to get ready for a long trip." The minister chuckled, "I know what you mean. It's the same in my business."

A father was approached by his small son who told him proudly, "I know what the Bible means!" His father smiled and replied, :What do you mean, you 'know' what the Bible means?" The son replied, "I do know!" "Okay," said his father. "What does the Bible mean?" "That's easy, Daddy," the young boy replied excitedly. "It stands for 'Basic Information Before Leaving Earth.'"

Sunday after church, a Mom asked her very young daughter what the lesson was about. The daughter answered, "Don't be scared, you'll get your quilt." Needless to say, the Mom was perplexed. Later in the day, the pastor stopped by for tea and the Mom asked him what that morning's Sunday school lesson was about. He said "Be not afraid, thy comforter is coming."

The minister was preoccupied with thoughts of how he was going to ask the congregation to come up with more money than they were expecting for repairs to the church building. Therefore, he was annoyed to find that the regular organist was sick and a substitute had been brought in at the last minute. The substitute wanted to know what to play. "Here's a copy of the service," he said impatiently. "But, you'll have to think of something to play after I make the announcement about the finances." During the service, the minister paused and said, "Brothers and Sisters, we are in great difficulty; the roof repairs cost twice as much as we expected and we need $4,000 more. Any of you who can pledge $100 or more, please stand up." At that moment, the substitute organist played "The Star Spangled Banner." And that is how the substitute became the regular organist!

Redneck Valentine Poem

Collards is green,
My dog's name if Blue
And I'm so lucky
To have a sweet thang like you.

Yore hair is like cornsilk
a-flapping in the breeze.
Softer than Blue's
And without all them fleas.

You move like the bass,
Which excite me in May.
You ain't got no scales
But I luv you anyway.

Yo're as satisfy'n as okry
Jist a-fry'n in the pan.
Yo're as fragrant as "snuff"
Right out of the can.

You have some'a yore teeth,
For which I am proud;
I hold my head high
When we're in a crowd.

On special occasions,
When you shave under yore arms,
Well, I'm in hawg heaven,
And awed by yore charms.

Still them fellers at work,
They all want to know,
What I did to deserve
Such a purdy, young doe.

Like a good roll of duct tape
Yo're there fer yore man,
To patch up life's troubles
And fix what you can.

Yo"re as cute as a junebug
a-buzzin' overhead.
You ain't mean like those fat ants
I found in my bed.

Cut from the best cloth
Like a plaid flannel shirt,
You spark up my life
More than a fresh load of dirt.

When you hold me real tight
Like a padded gunrack,
My life is complete;
Ain't nuttin' I lack.

Yore complexion, it's perfection,
Like the best vinyl sidin'.
Despite all the years,
Yore age, it keeps hidin'.

Me 'n' you's like a Moon Pie
With a RC cold drank,
We go together
Like a skunk goes with stank.

Some men, they buy chocolate
For Valentine's Day;
They git it at Wal-Mart,
It's romantic that way.

Some men git roses
On that special day
From the cooler at Kroger.
"That's impressive," I say.
Some men buy fine diamonds
From a flea market booth.

"Diamonds are forever,"
They explain, suave and couth.

But for this man, honey,
These won't do.
Cause yor'e too special,
You sweet thang you.

I got you a gift,
Without taste nore odor
More useful than diamonds…
IT'S A NEW TROLL'N MOTOR

Happy Valentines Day


A senior citizen in Florida bought a brand new Mercedes convertible. He took off down the road, flooring it to 80 mph and enjoying the wind blowing through what little hair he had left on his head. "This is great," he thought as he roared down I-75. He pushed the pedal to the metal even more. Then he looked in his rear view mirror and saw a highway patrol trooper behind him, blue lights flashing and siren blaring. "I can get away from him with no problem" thought the man and he tromped it some more and flew down the road at over 100 mph. Then 100, 120 mph! Then he thought, "What am I doing? I'm too old for this kind of think.' He pulled over to the side of the road and waited for the trooper to catch up with him. The trooper pulled in behind the Mercedes and walked up to the man "Sir," he said, looking at his watch. "My shift ends in 30 minutes and today is Friday. If you can give me a reason why you were speeding that I've never heard before, I'll let you go." The man looked at the trooper and said, "Years ago my wife ran off with a Florida state trooper, and I thought you were bringing her back." The trooper replied, "Sir, have a nice day."

Senator Hillary Clinton visits a primary school in New York to talk about the world. After her talk, she has a "question and answer" period. A little boy raises his hand and the senator asks him for his name. "Kenneth," he answered. "And what is your question, Kenneth?" asked Senator Clinton. "I have three questions: First, whatever happened to your medical health care plan? Second, why would you consider running for President after your husband shamed the office? And third, whatever happened to all those things you took when you left the White House?" Just then the bell rings for recess. Hillary Clinton informs the children that they will continue after recess. When they resume Hillary says, "Okay where were we? Oh, that's right, question time. Who has a question?" A different boy puts his hand up. Hillary points to him and asks him for his name. "Larry," he answered. "And what is your question Larry?" asked Hillary. I have five questions: First, whatever happened to your medical health care plan? Second, why would you consider running for President after your husband shamed the office? Third, whatever happened to all those things you took when you left the White House? Fourth, why did the recess bell go off 20 minutes early? And five, what happened to Kenneth?"

A man takes the day off work and decided to go out golfing. He is on the second hole when he notices a frog sitting next to the green. He thinks nothing of it and is about to shoot when he hears, "Ribbit 9 Iron." The man looks around and doesn't see anyone. Again, he hears, "Ribbit 9 Iron." He looks at the frog and decides to prove the frog wrong, puts the club away and grabs a 9 iron. Boom! He hits it 10 inches from the cup. He is shocked. He says to the frog, "Wow that's amazing. You must be a lucky frog, eh?" The frog replies, "Ribbit Lucky frog." The man decides to take the frog with him to the next hole. "What do you think frog?" the man asks. "Ribbit 3 wood." The guy takes out a 3 wood and Boom! Hole in one. The man is befuddled and doesn't know what to say. By the end of the day, the man golfed the best game of golf in his life and asks the frog, "Ok where to next?" The frog replies, "Ribbit Las Vegas." They go to Las Vegas and the guy says, "Ok frog, now what?" The frog says, "Ribbit roulette." Upon approaching the roulette table, the man asks, "What do you think I should bet?" The frog replies, "Ribbit $3000, black 6."

Now, this is a million-to-one shot to win, but after the golf game the man figures what the heck. Boom! Tons of cash comes sliding back across the table. The man takes his winnings and buys the best room in the hotel. He sits the frog down and says, "Frog, I don't know how to repay you. You've won me all this money and I am forever grateful." The frog replies, "Ribbit Kiss Me." He figures why not, since after all the frog did for him, he deserves it. With a kiss, the frog turns into a gorgeous 15-year-old girl. "And that, your honor, is how the girl ended up in my room. So help me God or my name is not William Jefferson Clinton."

Irish Prostitute

An Irish daughter had not been home for over 5 years. Upon her return, her father cussed her. "Where have ye been all this time? Why did ye not write to us, not even a line? Why didn't ye call? Can ye not understand what ye put yer old mum thru? The girl, crying, replied, "Sniff, sniff…dad…I became a prostitute…" "Ye what!!? Out of here, ye shameless harlot! Sinner! You're a disgrace to this family." "Ok, dad – as you wish. I just came back to give mum this luxurious fur coat, title deed to a ten bedroom mansion plus a savings certificate for $5 million. For me little brother, this gold Rolex and for ye daddy, the sparkling new Mercedes limited edition convertible that's parked outside plus a membership to the country club…(takes a breath)… and an invitation for ya all to spend New Years Eve on board my new yacht in the Riviera, and…" "Now what was it ye said ye had become?" says dad. Girl, crying again, "Sniff, sniff…a prostitute dad! Sniff, sniff." "Oh Be Jesus! Ye scared me half to death, girl! I thought ye said a Protestant. Come here and give yer old man a hug!"

A New Orleans lawyer sought an F.H.A. loan for a client. He was told the loan would be granted if he could prove satisfactory title to a parcel of property being offered as collateral. The title to the property dated back to 1803, which took the lawyer three months to track down. After sending the information to the F.H.A., he received the following reply (actual letter): "Upon review of your letter adjoining your client's loan application, we note that the request is supported by an Abstract of Title. While we compliment the able manner in which you have prepared and presented the application, we must point out that you have only cleared title to the proposed collateral property back to 1803. Before final approval can be accorded, it will be necessary to clear the title back to its origin." Annoyed the lawyer responded as follows (actual letter): "Your letter regarding title in Case NO. 189156 has been received. I note that you wish to have title extended further than the 194 years covered by the present application. I was unaware that nay educated person in this country, particularly those working in the property area, would not know that Louisiana was purchased by the U.S. from France in 1803, the year of origin identified in our application. For the edification of uninformed F.H.A. bureaucrats, the title to the land prior to U.S. ownership was obtained from France, which had acquired it by Right of Conquest from Spain. The land came into possession of Spain by Right of Discovery made in the year 1492 by a sea captain named Christopher Columbus, who had been granted the privilege of seeking a new route to India by the then reigning monarch, Isabella. The good queen, being a pious woman and careful about titles, almost as much as the F.H.A. took the precatution of securing the blessing of the Pope before she sold her jewels to fund Columbus' expedition. Now the Pope, as I'm sure you know, is the emissary of Jesus Christ, the Son of God. And God, it is commonly accepted, created this world. Therefore, I believe it is safe to presume that He also made that part of the World called Louisiana. He therefore, would be the owner of origin. I hope to hell you find His original claim to be satisfactory. Now, may we have our damn loan? They got it.

## DUI WV Style

Only a West Virginian could think of this…from the county where drunk driving is considered a sport, comes this true story. Recently a routine police patrol parked outside a bar in Ripley, WV. After last call the officer noticed a man leaving the bar so intoxicated that he could barely walk. The man stumbled around the parking a lot for a few minutes, with the officer quietly observing. After what seemed an eternity and trying his keys on five different vehicles, the man managed to find his car which he fell into. He sat there for a few minutes as a number of other patrons left the bar and drove off. Finally he started the car, switched the wipers on and off (it was a fine, dry summer night) – flicked the blinkers on, then off a couple of times, honked the horn and then switched on the lights. He moved the vehicle forward a few inches, reversed a little and then remained still for a few more minutes as some more of the other patron vehicles left. At last, the parking lot empty, he pulled out of the parking lot and started to drive slowly down the road. The police officer, having patiently waited all this time, now started up the patrol car, put on the flashing lights, and promptly pulled the man over and carried out a Breathalyzer test. To his amazement the Breathalyzer indicated no evidence of the man having consumed any alcohol at all! Dumbfounded, the officer said, "I'll have to ask you to accompany me to the police station. This Breathalyzer equipment must be broken." "I doubt I," said the truly proud Hillbilly. "Tonight I'm the designated decoy."

John O'Reilly hoisted his beer and said, "Here's to spending the rest of me life, between the legs of me wife!" That won him the top prize at the pub for the best toast of the night! He went home and told his wife, Mary, "I won the prize for the best toast of the night." She said, "Aye, did ye now. And what was your toast?" John said, "Here's to spending the rest of me life, in church with me wife." "Oh, that is very nice indeed, John!" Mary said. The next day, Mary ran into one of John's drinking buddies on the street corner. The man chuckled leeringly and said, "John won the prize the other night at the pub with a toast about you, Mary." She said, "Aye, he told me, and I was a bit surprised meself. You know, he's only been there twice in the last four years. Once he fell asleep, and the other time I had to pull him by the ears to make him come."

True Friendship

When you are sad – I will help get you drunk and plot revenge against the sorry bastard who made you sad.
When you are blue – I will try to dislodge whatever is choking you.

When you smile – I will know you finally got laid.

When you are scared – I will rag on you about it every chance I get.

When you are worried – I will tell you horrible stories about how much worse it could be and to quit whining.

When you are confused – I will use little words.

When you are sick – Stay the hell away from me until you are well again. I don't want whatever you have.

When you fall – I will point and laugh at your clumsy ass.

This is my oath. I pledge it till the end. Why, you may ask?

Because you are my friend.

Remember:

A good friend will help you move.

A really good friend will help you move a body.

Let me know if I ever need to bring a shovel.

Tower: "Delta 351, you have traffic at 10 o'clock, 6 miles!"

Delta 351: Give us another hint, we have digital watches."

O'hare Approach Control to a 747: "United 329 heavy, your traffic is a Fokker, one o'clock, three miles eastbound.

United 329: Approach I've always wanted to say this…I've got the little Fokker in sight."

A student became lost during a solo cross-country flight. While attempting to locate the aircraft on radar, ATC asked, "What was your last known position?" Student: "When I was number one for take-off."

One day the pilot of a Cherokee 180 was told by the tower to hold short of the active runway while a DC-8 landed. The DC-8 landed, rolled out, turned around and taxied back past the Cherokee. Some quick-witted comedian in the DC-8 crew got on the radio and said, "What a cute little plane, did you make it all by yourself?" The Cherokee pilot, not about to let the insult go by, came back with a real zinger: "I made it out of DC-8 parts. Another landing like yours and I"ll have enough parts for another one."

"TWA 2341, for the noise abatement turn right 45 degrees." "Centre, we are at 35,000 feet. How much noise can we make up here?" "Sir, have you ever heard the noise a 747 makes when it hits a 727?"

A flight attendant was stationed at the departure gate to check tickets. As a man approached, she extended her hand for the ticket, he opened his coat and flashed her. Not missing a beat, she said, "Sir, I need to see your ticket, not your stub."

## NEWSPAPERS

Free Yorkshire Terrier. 8 years old. Hateful little dog. Bites

Free Puppies..Part Shepherd, part stupid dog

German Shepherd 85 lbs. Neutered. Speaks German. Free

Found: Dirty White Dog. Looks like a rat..been out awhile.

Disturbing Beer News: Yesterday, University scientists released the results of a recent analysis that revealed the presence of female hormones in beer. Men should take a concerned look at their beer consumption. The theory is that beer contains female hormones (hops contain phytoestrogens) and that by drinking enough beer, men turn into women. To test the theory, 100 men were fed 8 pints of beer each wintin a 1 hour perior. It was then observed that 100% of the test subjects:
1. Gained weight.
2. Talked excessively without making sense.
3. Became overly emotional.
4. Couldn't drive.
5. Failed to think rationally.
6. Argued over nothing.
7. Had to sit down while urinating.
8. Refused to apologize when obviously wrong.

No further testing was considered necessary.

Four friends, who hadn't seen each other in 30 years, reunited at a party. After several drinks, one of the men had to use the restroom. Those who remained talked about their kids. The first guy said, "My son is my pride and joy. He started working at a successful company at the bottom of the barrel. He studied Economics and Business Administration and soon began to climb the corporate ladder and not he's the president of the company. He became so rich that he gave his best friend a top of the line Mercedes for his birthday." The second guy said, "Damn, that's terrific! My son is also my pride and joy. He started working for a big airline, then went to flight school to become a pilot. Eventually he became a partner in the company, where he owns the majority of its assets. He's so rich that he gave his best friend a brand new jet for his birthday." The third man said" "Well, that's terrific! My son studied in the universities and became an engineer. Then he started his own construction company and is now a multimillionaire. He also gave away something very nice and expensive to his best friend for his birthday: a 30,000 square foot mansion." The three friends congratulated each other just as the fourth returned from the restroom and asked: "What are all the congratulations for?" One of the three said: "We are talking about the pride we feel for the successes of our sons. What about your son?" The fourth man replied: "My son is gay and makes a living dancing as a stripper at a nightclub." The three friends said: "What a shame…what a disappointment." The fourth man replied: "No, I'm not ashamed. He's my son and I love him. And he's lucky, too. His birthday just passed and the other day he received a beautiful 30,000 square foot mansion, a brand new jet and a top of the line Mercedes from his three boyfriends."

Fairy Tales for Girls

This is the fairy tale that we should have been reading as little girls. Once upon a time, in a land far away, a beautiful, independent, self-assured princess happened upon a frog as she sat, contemplating ecological issues on the shores of an unpolluted pond in a verdant meadow near her castle. The frog hopped into the princess'lap and said: Elegant Lady, I was once a handsome prince, until an evil witch cast a spell upon me. One kiss from you, however, and I will turn back into the dapper, young prince that I am and then, my sweet, we can marry and set up housekeeping in your castle with my mother, where you can prepare my meals, clean my clothes, bear my children and forever feel grateful and happy doing so. That night as the princess dined sumptuously on lightly sautéed frog legs seasoned in a white wine and onion cream sauce, she chuckled and thought to herself: I DO NOT think so.

An old man lived alone in the country. He wanted to dig his potato garden but it was very hard work as the ground was hard. His only son Fred, who use to help him, was in prison. The old man wrote a letter to his son and described his predicament.

Dear Fred, I am feeling pretty bad because it looks like I won't be able to plant my potato garden this year. I'm just getting too old to be digging up a garden plot. If you were here, all my troubles would be over. I know you would dig the plot for me. Love, Dad

A few days later he received a letter from his son.

Dear Dad, For heaven's sake, don't dig up that garden! That's where I buried the BODIES. Love, Fred

At 4 am the next morning, FBI agents and local police arrived and dug up the entire area without finding any bodies. They apologized to the old man and left.

That same day the old man received another letter from his son.

Dear Dad, Go ahead and plant the potatoes now. That's the best I could do under the circumstances. Love, Fred

A photographer from a well-known national magazine was assigned to cover the recent Southern California fires. The magazine wanted to show some of the heroic work of the firefighters as they battled the blazes. When the photographer arrived, he realized that the smoke was so thick that it would seriously impede or make it impossible for him to photograph anything from grand-level. So he requested permission to rent a plane and take photos from the air. His request was approved, and arrangements were made. He was told to report to a nearby airport, where a single-engine plane would be waiting for him. He arrived at the airport and saw a plane warming up near the gate. He jumped in with his bag and shouted. "Let's go!" The pilot swung the plane into the wind, and within minutes they were in the air. The photographer said, "Fly over the park and make two or three low passes so I can take some picture." "Why?" asked the pilot. "Because I am a photographer for a national magazine," he responded, "and I need some close-up shots." The pilot was silent for a moment, finally he stammered, "So, you're telling me you're not the flight instructor?"

COWS, CALVES NEVER BRED…Also 1 gay bull for sale

NORDIC TRACK $300 Hardly used, call Chubby

GEORGIA PEACHES, California grown – 89 cents lb.

NICE PARACHUTE: Never opened – used once

JOING NUDIST COLONY! Must sell washer and dryer $300

WEDDING DRESS FOR SALE. WORN ONCE BY MISTAKE. Call Stephanie.

FOR SALE BY OWNER: Complete set of Encyclopedia Britannica. 45 volumes. Excellent condition!! $10 or best offer. No longer needed. Got married last month. Freak'ng wife knows everything.

How to Install a Wireless Security System

Go to a second-hand store, buy a pair of men's used work boots, a really big pair. Put them outside your front door on top of a copy of Guns and Ammo magazine. Put a dog dish beside it. A really big dish. Leave a note on your front door that says something like "Bubba, me and big Mike have gone to get more ammunition—back in ½ an hour. Don't disturb the pit bulls, they've just been wormed."

## Exercise for People Over 50

Begin by standing on a comfortable surface, where you have plenty of room at each side. With a 5-lb potato sack in each hand, extend your arms straight out from your sides and hold them there as long as you can. Try to reach a full minute, and then relax. Each day you'll find that you can hold this position for just a bit longer. After a couple of weeks, move up to 10-lb potato sacks. Then try 50-lb potato sacks and then eventually try to get to where you can lift a 100-lb potato sack in each hand and hold your arms straight for more that a full minute (I'm at this level). After you feel confident at that level, put a potato in each sack.

Another way to pull off a Sunday afternoon quickie with their 8 year old son in the apartment was to send him out on the balcony with a Popsicle and tell him to report on all the neighborhood activities. He began his commentary as his parents put their plan into operation: "There's a car being towed from the parking lot", he shouted. A few moments passed…"An ambulance just drove by." A few moments later, "Looks like the Anderson's have company," he called out. "Matt's riding a new bike." A few moments later "Looks like the Sanders are moving. Jason is on his skate board…" A few more moments, "The Coppers are having sex!!" Startled, his Mother and Dad shop up in bed! Dad cautiously called out, "How do you know they are having sec?" "Jimmy Cooper's standing on his balcony with a Popsicle too."

An 80 year old guy goes to the doctor for a check-up. The doctor is amazed at what good shape the guy is in and asks, "How do you stay in such great physical shape?" "I'm a golfer," says the old guy, "and that's why I'm in such good shape. I'm up well before daylight and out golfing up and down the fairways." "Well," said the doctor, "I'm sure that helps, but there's got to be more to it than that. How old was your dad when he died?" "Who said my dad's dead?" The doctor is amazed, "you mean you're 80 years old and your dad's still alive?

How old is he?" "He's 100 years old," said the old golfer, "in fact, he golfed with me this morning and that's why he's still alive…he's a golfer too." "Well," the doctor said, "that's great, but I'm sure there's got to be more to it than that. How about your dad's dad? How old was he when he died?" "Who said my grandpa's dead?" Stunned, the doctor asks, "You mean you're 80 years old and your grandfather's still living? Just how old is he anyway?" "He's 118 years old," said the old golfer. The doctor is getting frustrated at this point and says, "So, I guess he went golfing with you this morning too?" "No…Grandpa couldn't go this morning because he got married." The doctor can hardly believe it. "Got married!!! Why in the hell would a 118 year old guy want to get married?" "Who said he wanted to?"

A father put his three year old daughter to bed, told her a story and listened to her prayers which she ended by saying: "God bless Mommy, God bless Daddy, God bless Grandma and good-bye Grandpa." The father asked, "Why did you say good-bye grandpa?" The little girl said, "I don't know daddy, it just seemed like the thing to do." The next day grandpa died. The father thought it was a strange coincidence. A few months later the father put the girl to bed and listened to her prayers which went like this" "God bless Mommy, God Bless Daddy and good-bye Grandma." The next day the grandmother died. Oh my gosh, thought the father, this kid is in contact with the other side. Several weeks later when the girl was going to bed the dad heard her say: "God bless Mommy and good-bye Daddy." He practically went into shock. He couldn't sleep all night and got up at the crack of dawn to go to his office. He was nervous as a cat all day, had lunch sent in and watched the clock. He figured if he could get by until midnight he would be okay. He felt safe in the office, so instead of going home at the end of the day he stayed there, drinking coffee, looking at his watch and jumping at every sound. Finally midnight arrived, he breathed a sign of relief and went home. When he got home his wife said "I've never seen you work so late, what's the matter?" He said "I don't want to talk about it, I've just spent the worst day of my life." She said "You think you had a bad day, you'll never believe what happened to me. This morning the milkman dropped dead on our porch."

The coach was addressing a little boy on his team. "Son, do you know what a team is?" The little boy nodded in the affirmative. "Do you understand that what matters is whether we win or lose together as a team?" The little boy nodded yes. "So," the coach continued, "I'm sure you know, when an out is called, you shouldn't argue, curse, attack the umpire or call him a peckerhead. Do you understand all that?" Again the little boy nodded. He continued, "And when I take you out of the game so another boy gets a chance to play, it's not good sportsmanship to call your coach a dumb @sshole, is it?" Again the little boy nodded. "Good," said the coach. "Now go over there and explain all that to your grandmother."

Deer Sir, I waunt to apply for the secritary job what I saw in the paper. I can Type real quik wit one finggar and do sum a counting. I think I am good on the phone and no I am a pepole person, Pepole really seam to respond to me well. Im lookin for a Jobb as a secritary but it musent be to complicaited. I no my spelling is not to good but find that I offen can get a job thru my persinalety. My salerery is open so we can discus wat you want to pay me and wat you think that I am werth, I can start imeditely. Thank you in advanse fore yore anser. Hopifuly Yore best applicant so farr.
Sinseerly, Peggy May Starlings

Amazingly Simple Home Remedies
1. If you are choking on an ice cube, don't panic. Simply pour a cup of boiling water down your throat and presto. The blockage will be almost instantly removed.
2. Clumsy? Avoid cutting yourself while slicing vegetables by getting someone else to hold them while you chop away.
3. Avoid arguments with the Mrs. About lifting the toilet seat by simply using the sink.
4. For high blood pressure sufferers: simply cut yourself and bleed for few minutes, thus reducing the pressure in your veins. Remember to use timer.

5. A mouse trap, places on top of your alarm clock will prevent you from rolling over and going back to sleep after you hit the snooze button.
6. If you have a bad cough, take a large does of laxatives, then you will be afraid to cough.
7. Have a bad toothache? Smash your thumb with a hammer and you will forget about the toothache.

Sometimes, we just need to remember what the rules of life really are:

You only need two tools: WD-40 and Duct Tape. If it doesn't move and should, use the WD-40. If it shouldn't move and does, use the duct tape.

Remember: Everyone seems normal until you get to know them.

Never pass up an opportunity to go to the bathroom.

If you woke up breathing, congratulations! You get another chance.

And finally, be really nice to your family and friends; you never know when you might need them to empty your bedpan.

## LEFT BRAIN/RIGHT BRAIN

While sitting at your desk, lift your right foot off the floor and make clockwise circles. Now, while doing this, draw the number 6 in the air with your right hand. Your foot will change direction and there's nothing you can do about it. WEIRDDDDDDD!!!

## I Own a Weedeater

South Texas farmers, Jim and Bob are sitting at their favorite bar drinking beer. Jim turns to Bob and says, "You know, I'm tired of going through life without an education. Tomorrow I think I'll go to the community college and sign up for some classes." Bob thinks it's a good idea, and the two leave. The next day Jim goes down to the college and meets the dean of admission, who signs him up for the four basic classes: Math, English, History and Logic. "Logic?" Jim says. "What's that?" The dean says, "I'll show you. Do you own a weedeater?" "Yeah." "Then logically because you own a weedeater, I think that you would have a yard." "That's true, I do have a yard." "I'm not done," the dean says. "Because you have a yard, I think logically that you would have a house." "Yes, I do have a house." "And because you have a house, I think that you might logically have a family." "I have a family." "I'm not done yet. Because you have a family, then logically you must have a wife." "Yes, I do have a wife." "And because you have a wife, then logically you must be a heterosexual." "I am a heterosexual. That's amazing, you were able to find out all of that because I have a weedeater." Excited to take the class now, Jim shakes the dean's hand and leaves to go meet Bob at the bar. He tells Bob about his classes, how he is signed up for Math, English, History and Logic. "Logic?" Bob says, "What's that?" Jim says, "I'll show you. Do you have a weekeater?" "No." "Then you're gay."

## BODY MEETING:

All the organs of the body were having a meeting, trying to decide who was the one in charge. "I should be in charge," said the brain, "because I run all the body's systems, so without me nothing would happen." "I should be in charge," said the blood, "because I circulate oxygen all over so without me you'd all waste away." "I should be in charge," said the stomach, "because I process food and give all of you energy." "I should be in charge," said the legs, "because I carry the body wherever it needs to go." "I should be in charge," said the eyes, "because I allow the body to see where it goes." "I should be in charge," said the rectum, "because I'm responsible for waste removal." All the other body parts laughed at the rectum and insulted him, so he shut down tight. Within a few days, the brain had a terrible headache, the stomach was bloated, the legs got wobbly, the eyes got watery, and the blood was toxic. They all decided that the rectum should be the boss. The moral of the story? The asshole is usually in charge!!

An 80 year old woman was arrested for shop lifting. When she went before the judge he asked her, "What did you steal?" She replied, "A can of peaches." The judge asked her why she had stolen them and she replied that she was hungry. The judge then asked her how many peaches were in the can. She replied "6". The judge then said, "I will give you 6 days in jail." Before the judge could actually pronounce the punishment, the woman's husband spoke up and asked the judge if he could say something. The judge said, "What is it?" The husband said, "She also stole a can of peas."

One beautiful December evening Pedro and his girlfriend Rosita were sitting by the side of the ocean. It was a romantic full moon, when Pedro said, "Hey, mamacita, let's play Weeweechu." "Oh no, not now, let's look at the moon" said Rosita. "Oh c'mon baby, let's you and I play Weeweechu. I love you and it's the perfect time," Pedro begged. "But I wanna just hold your hand and watch the moon." "Please, corazoncito, just once, play Weeweechu with me." Rosita looked at Pedro and said, "Ok, one time, we'll play Weeweechu." Pedro grabbed his guitar and they both sang... "Weeweechu a Merry Christmas, Weeweechu a Merry Christmas, Weeweechu a Merry Christmas and a Happy New Year."

## Do Not Lose Your Grandkids in the Mall!

A small boy was lost at a large shopping mall. He approached a uniformed policeman and said, "I've lost my grandpa!" The cop asked, "What's he like?" The little boy replied, "Jack Daniels and women with big breasts."

## The Dead Goldfish

Little Carol was in the garden filling in a hole when her neighbor peered over the fence. Interested in what the cheeky-faced youngster was doing, he asked, "What are you up to there, Carol?" "My goldfish is dead," replied Carol tearfully, without looking up, "and I've just buried him." The neighbor laughed, and said condescendingly, "That's a really big hole for a goldfish, isn't it?" Carol patted down the last heap of earth then replied, "That's because he's inside your damn cat."

## A Smart Old Rancher

The Texas Department of Water representative stopped at a ranch and talked with an old rancher. He told the rancher, "I need to inspect your ranch for your water allocation." The old rancher said, "Okay, but don't go in that field over there." The water representative said, "Mister, I have the authority of the Federal Government with me. See this card? This card means I am allowed to go WHEREVER I WISH on any agricultural land. No questions asked or answered. Have I made myself clear? Do you understand?" The old rancher nodded politely and went about his chores. Later, the old rancher heard loud screams and saw the water representative running for the fence and close behind was the rancher's bull. The bull was gaining on the water representative with every step. The rep was clearly terrified, so the old rancher immediately threw down his tools, ran to the fence and shouted out.... "Your card! Your card! Show him your card."

## Fido

A young Southern boy goes off to college, but about 1/3 way through the semester, he has foolishly squandered what money his parents gave him. Then he gets an idea. He calls his Redneck father. "Dad, he says, "you won't believe the wonders that modern education are coming up with! Why, they actually have a program here that will teach Fido how to talk!" "That's absolutely amazing! His father says. "How do I get him in that program?" "Just send him down here with $1000," the boy says, "I'll get him into the course." So, his father sends the dog and the $1000. About 2/3 way through the semester, the money runs out. The boy calls his father again. "So, how's Fido doing, son?" his father asks. "Awesome, dad he's talking up a storm," he says, "but you just won't believe this – they've had such good results with this program, that they've implemented a new one to teach the animals how to READ!" "READ!?" says his father, "No kidding! What do I have to do to get him in that program?" "Just send $2,500, I'll get him in the class." His father sends the money. The boy has a problem. At the end of the year, his father will find out that the dog can neither talk nor read. So he shoots the dog. When he gets home, his father is all excited. "Where's Fido? I just can't wait to see him talk and read something!" "Dad," the boy says, "I have some grim news. This morning, when I got out of the shower, Fido was in the living room kicking back in the recliner, reading the morning paper, like he usually does. Then he turned to me and asked, "So, is your daddy still messin' around with that little redhead who lives on Oak Street?" The father says, "I hope you SHOT that lyin' son of a bitch!" "I sure did Dad." "That's my boy."

A young family moved into a house next door to a vacant lot. One day a construction crew turned up to start building a house on the empty lot. The young family's 5-year old daughter naturally took an interest in all the activity going on next-door and spent much of each day observing the workers. Eventually, the construction crew, all of them gems-in-in-the-rough, more or less adopted her as a kind of project mascot. They chatted with her, let her sit with them while they had coffee and lunch breaks, and gave her little jobs to do here and there to make her feel important. At the end of the first week they even presented her with a pay envelope containing a couple of dollars. The little girl took this home to her mother who said all the appropriate words of admiration and suggested they take the two-dollar "pay" she had received to the bank the next day to start a savings account. When the girl got to the bank, the teller was equally impressed and asked the little girl how she had come by her very own paycheck at such a young age. The little girl proudly replied, "I worked last week with the crew building the house next door to us." "My goodness gracious," said the teller, "and will you be working on the house again this week, too?" The little girl replied, "I will if those assholes at Home Depot ever deliver the @*&#* sheet rock..." Kind of brings a tear to the eye....

If you ever testify in court, you might wish you could have been as sharp as this policeman. He was being cross-examined by a defense attorney during a felony trial. The lawyer was trying to undermine the policeman's credibility... Q: "Officer – did you see my client fleeing the scene?" A: "No sir. But I subsequently observed a person matching the description of the offender, running several blocks away." Q: "Officer—who provided this description?" A: "The officer who responded to the scene." Q: "A fellow officer provided the description of this so-called offender. Do you trust your fellow officers?" A: "yes, sir. With my life." Q: "With your life? Let me ask you this then officer. Do you have a room where you change your clothes in preparation for your daily duties?" A: "Yes sir, we do!" Q: "And do you have a locker in the room?" A: "Yes sir, I do." Q: "And do you have a lock on your locker?" A: "Yes sir." Q: "Now why is it, officer, if you trust your fellow officers with your life, you find it necessary to lock your locker in a room you share with these same officers?" A: "You see, sir —we share the building with the court complex, and sometimes lawyers have been known to walk through that room." The courtroom EXPLODED with laughter, and a prompt recess was called. The officer on the stand has been nominated for this year's "Best Comeback" line and we think he'll win.

## Never Underestimate a Redneck

A Redneck from Alabama walked into a bank in New York City and asked for the loan officer. He told the loan officer that he was going to Bakersfield on business for two weeks and needed to borrow $5,000 and that he was not a depositor of the bank. The bank officer told him that the bank would need some form of security for the loan, so the Redneck handed over the keys to a new Ferrari. The car was parked on the street in front of the bank. The Redneck produced the title and everything checked out. The loan officer agreed to hold the car as collateral for the loan and apologized for having to charge 12% interest. Later, the bank's president and its officers all enjoyed a good laugh at the Redneck from the south for using a $250,000 Ferrari as collateral for a $5,000 loan. An employee of the bank then drove the Ferrari into the bank's private underground garage and parked it. Two weeks later, the Redneck returned, repaid the $5,000 and the interest of $23.07. The loan officer said, "Sir, we are very happy to have had your business, and this transaction has worked out very nicely, but we are a little puzzled. While you were away, we checked you out and found that you are a multimillionaire. What puzzles us is, why would you bother to borrow $5,000?" The gold "ole Alabama boy replied, "Where else in New York City can I park my car for two weeks for only $23.07 and expect it to be there when I return?" His name was Bubba.

## Only a Mexican Wife

The sick Mexican husband was lying on his death bed. He had only hours to live when suddenly he smelled tamales. He dearly loved tamales more than anything else in the world, especially his wife Chita's tamales. With his last bit of the energy left in his mind and body, the terminal husband pulled himself out of bed, across the floor, down the hall and into the kitchen. Here, his wife was removing the batch of tamales from the stove top. As he reached for one of the freshly made tamales, his wife, Chita, smacked him in the back of the head with a wooden spoon, "Leave them alone pendejo!.... They're for the funeral!"

The Lone Ranger and Tonto went camping in the desert. After they got their tent all set up, both men fell sound asleep. Some hours later, Tonto wakes the Lone Ranger and says, "Kemo Sabe, look towards sky, what you see?" The Lone Ranger replied, "I see millions of stars." "What that tell you?" asked Tonto. The Lone Ranger ponders for a minute then says, "Astronomically speaking, it tells me there are millions of galaxies and potentially billions of planets. Astrologically, it tells me that Satrun is in Leo. Time wide, it appears to be approximately a quarter past three in the morning. Theologically, the Lord is all-powerful and we are small and insignificant. Meterologically, it seems we will have a beautiful day tomorrow. What's it tell you, Tonto?" "You dumber that buffalopooh. It means someone stole the tent."

## Letter to My Bank

Dear Sirs, In view of current development in the banking market, one of my checks was returned marked "insufficient funds". Does that refer to me or to you? Sincerely Yours

An Old Native Chief sat in his hut on the reservation, smoking a ceremonial pipe and eyeing two government officials sent to interview him. Chief Two Eagles asked one official, "You have observed the white man for 90 years. You've seen his wars and his technological advances. You've seen his progress, and the damage he's done." The chief nodded in agreement. The official continued, "Considering all these events in your opinion, where did the white man go wrong?" The Chief stared at the government officials for over a minute and then calmly replied, "When white man found the land, Natives were running it. No taxes. No debt. Plenty buffalo. Plenty beaver. Women did all the work. Medicine man free. Indian man spent all day hunting and fishing and all night having sex." Then the Chief leaned back and smiled, "Only white man dumb enough to think he could improve system like that."

A Very Good Example of the Kind of Representation We Have in Congress

A noted psychiatrist was a guest speaker at an academic function where Nancy Pelosi happened to appear. Ms. Pelosi took the opportunity to schmooze the good doctor a bit and asked him a question with which he was most at ease. "Would you mind telling me, Doctor," she asked, "how do you detect a mental deficiency in somebody who appears completely normal?" "Nothing is easier," he replied. "You ask a simple question which anyone should answer with no trouble. If the person hesitates, that puts you on the track." "What sort of question?" asked Pelosi. "Well, you might ask, Captain Cook made three trips around the world and died during one of them, which one?" Pelosi thought a moment, and then said with a nervous laugh, "You wouldn't happen to have another example would you? I must confess I don't know much about history."

A birth certificate shows that we were born. A death certificate shows that we died. Pictures show that we lived!

I believe that just because two people argue, it doesn't mean they don't love each other. And just because they don't argue, it doesn't mean they do love each other. I believe that we don't have to change friends if we understand that friends change. I believe that no matter how good a friend is, they're going to hurt you every once in a while and you must forgive them for that. I believe that true friendship continues to grow, even over the longest distance. Same goes for true love. I believe that you can do something in an instant that will give you heartache for life. I believe that it's taking me a long time to become the person I want to be. I believe that you should always leave loved ones with loving words. It may be the last time you see them. I believe that you can keep going long after you think you can't. I believe that we are responsible for what we do, no matter how we feel. I believe that either you control your attitude or it controls you. I believe that heroes are the people who do what has to be done when it needs to be done, regardless of the consequences. I believe that money is a louse way of keeping score. I believe that my best friend and I can do anything or nothing and have the best time. I believe that sometimes the people you expect to kick you when you're down will be the ones to help you get back up. I believe that sometimes when I'm angry I have the right to be angry, but that doesn't give me the right to be cruel. I believe that maturity has more to do with what types of experiences you've had and what you've learned from them and less to do with how many birthdays you've celebrated. I believe that it isn't always enough to be forgiven by others. Sometimes, you have to learn to forgive yourself. I believe that no matter how bad your heart is broken the world doesn't stop for your grief. I believe that our background and circumstances may have influenced who we are, but, we are responsible for who we become. I believe that you shouldn't be so eager to find out a secret. It could change your life forever. I believe two people can look at the exact same thing and see something totally different. I believe that your life can be changed in a matter of hours by people who don't even know you. I believe that even when you think you have no more to give, when a friend cries out to you, you will find the strength to help. I believe the credentials on the wall do not make you a decent human being. I believe that the people you care about most in life are taken from you too soon. The happiest of people don't necessarily have the best of everything; they just make the most of everything.

Grandma and Grandpa were visiting their kids overnight. When Grandpa found a bottle of Viagra in his son's medicine cabinet, he asked about using one of the pills. The son said, "I don't think you should take one Dad; they're very strong and very expensive." "How much?" asked Grandpa. "$10.00 a pill," answered the son. "I don't care," said Grandpa, "I'd still like to try one, and before we leave in the morning, I'll put the money under the pillow." Later the next morning, the son found "$110.00 under the pillow. He called Grandpa and said, "I told you each pill was $10.00, not $110.00. "I know," said Grandpa. "The hundred is from Granma!"

## Why Parent Drink

A father passing by his son's bedroom was astonished to see that his bed was nicely made and everything was picked up. Then he saw an envelope, propped up prominently on the pillow that was addressed to "Dad." With the worst premonition he opened the envelope with trembling hands and read the letter. Dear Dad: It is with great regret and sorrow that I'm writing you. I had to elope with my new girlfriend because I wanted to avoid a scene with Mom and you. I have been finding real passion with Stacy and she is so nice. But I knew you would not approve of her because of all her piercing, tattoos, tight motorcycle clothes and the fact that she is much older than I am. But it's not only the passion…Dad she's pregnant. Stacy said that we will be very happy. She owns a trailer in the woods and has a stack of firewood for the whole winter. We share a dream of having many more children. Stacy has opened my eyes to the fact that marijuana doesn't really hurt anyone. We'll be growing it for ourselves and trading it with the other people that live nearby for cocaine and ecstasy. In the meantime we will pray that science will find a cure for AIDS so Stacy can get better. She deserves it. Don't worry Dad. I'm 15 and I know how to take care of myself. Someday I'm sure that we will be back to visit so that you can get to know your grandchildren. Love, Your Son John. PS Dad, none of the above is true. I'm over at Tommy's house. I just wanted to remind you that there are worse things in life than a report card that's in my center desk drawer. I love you. Call me when it's safe to come home.

## Where Would You Be?

If you had all the money your heart desires?
If you had the most fabulous home in the perfect neighborhood?
If you had no worries?
If you came home and the finest gourmet meal is waiting you?
If your bathwater had been run?
If you had the perfect kids?
If your partner was awaiting you with open arms and kisses?
So, where would you be?
Well hellooooo!!!! You'd be in the wrong damn house!

A man bumps into a woman in a hotel lobby and as he does, his elbow goes into her breast. They are both quite startled. The man turns to her and says, "Ma'am, if your heart is as soft as your breast, I know you'll forgive me." She replies, "If your penis is as hard as our elbow, I'm in room 221."

One night, as a couple lays down for bed, the husband starts rubbing his wife's arm. The wife turns over and says, "I'm sorry honey, I've got a gynecologist appointment tomorrow and I want to stay fresh." The husband, rejected, turns over. A few minutes later, he rolls back over and taps his wife again. "Do you have dentist appointment tomorrow too?"

Bill worked in a pickle factory. He had been employed there for a number o fyears when he came home one day to confess to his wife that he had a terrible compulsion. He had an urge to stick his penis into the pickle slicer. His wife suggested that he should see a sex therapist to talk about it, but Bill said he would be too embarrassed. He vowed to overcome the compulsion on his own. One day a few weeks later, Bill came home and his wife could see at once that something was seriously wrong. "What's wrong, Bill?" she asked. "Do you remember that I told you how I had this tremendous urge to put my penis into the pickle slicer?" "Oh, Bill, you didn't!" she exclaimed. "Yes, I did," he replied. "My God, Bill, what happened?" "I got fired." "No, Bill, I mean what happened with the pickle slicer?" "Oh…she got fired too."

A couple had been married for 50 years. They were sitting at the breakfast table one morning when the wife says, "Just think, fifty years ago we were sitting here at this breakfast table together. "I know," the old man said. "We were probably sitting here naked as a jaybird fifty years ago." "Well," Granny snickered. "Let's relive some old times." Where upon, the two stripped to the buff and sat down at the table. "You know, honey," the little old lady breathlessly replied, "my nipples are as hot for you today as they were fifty years ago." "I wouldn't be surprised," replied Gramps. One's in your coffee and the other is in your oatmeal."

10 Rules You Can Use

Rules of Golf for Good Players

1. On beginning play, as many balls as may be required to obtain a satisfactory results may be played from the first tee. Everyone recognizes a good player needs to "loosen up" but does not have time for practice tee.

2. A ball sliced or hooked in the rough shall be lifted and placed in the fairway at a point equal to the distance it carried or rolled in the rough. Such veering right or left frequently results from friction between the face of the club and the cover of the ball and the player should not be penalized for erratic behavior resulting from such uncontrollable mechanical performance.

3. A ball hitting a tree shall be deemed not to have hit the tree. Hitting a tree is simply bad luck and has no place in a scientific game. Players estimate the distance the ball would have traveled if it had not hit the tree and play the ball from there, preferably from atop a nice firm grass.

4. There shall be no such thing as a lost ball. Missing a ball is on or near the course somewhere and eventually will be found by someone else. It thus becomes a stolen ball, and the player should not compound the felony by charging himself with a penalty stroke.
5. When played from a sand trap, a ball which does not clear the trap on being stuck, may be hit again on the roll without counting any extra stroke. In no case, will more than two strokes be counted playing from a bunker, since it is only reasonable on his shot, instead of hurrying it, to keep pace with the group in front, he would be out in two.
6. If putt passes over hole without dropping, it is deemed to have dropped. The law of gravity holds that any object attempting to maintain a position in the atmosphere without something solid to support it must drop.
7. Same thing goes for a ball that stops at the lip of the hole and hangs there, defying gravity you cannot defy the law of gravity.
8. Rule #6 applies to any putt that rims around the cup. A round ball cannot go sideways, violates the law of physics, and the ball is deemed to have dropped into the cup.
9. If your opponent insists on assessing a stroke penalty for every ball that is hit and not found there should be reciprocity. You may in turn deduct a stroke from final score for each good ball that is found during your round.
10. A putt that stops close enough to the cup to inspire such comments as "you could blow it in" may in fact be blown in. This does not apply if the ball is more than three inches from the cup because no one wants to make travesty of the game.

Golf Etiquette; it is deemed to be rather impolite to inquire about another's score either during or after a round of golf. This could cause a golfer to falsify his actual score, and everyone knows, GOLFERS DON'T LIE.

Definition: GIMME – an agreement between two losers who can't putt.

Someone asked the other day, "What was your favorite fast food when you were growing up?" "We didn't have fast food when I was growing up," I informed him. "All the food was slow." "C'mon, seriously, where did you eat?" "It was a place called 'at home.'" I explained. "Mom cooked every day and Dad got home from work, we sat down together at the dining room table, and if I didn't like what she put on my plate I was allowed to sit there until I did like it." By this time, the kid was laughing so hard I was afraid he was going to suffer serious internal damage, so I didn't tell him the part about how I had to have permission to leave the table. But here are some other things I would have told him about my childhood if I figured his system could have handled it: Some parents NEVER! Owned their own house, wore Levis, set foot on a golf course, traveled out of the country or had a credit card. In their later years they had something called a revolving charge card. The card was good only at Sears & Roebuck. But there's no Roebuck anymore, maybe he died. My parents never drove me to soccer practice. This was mostly because we never had heard of soccer. I had a bicycle that weighed probably 50 pounds, and only had one speed, (slow). We didn't have a television in our house until I was 5. It was, of course, black and white. I was 13 before I tasted my first pizza, it was called 'pizza pie.' When I bit into it, I burned the roof of my mouth and the cheese slid off, swung down, plastered itself against my chin and burned that, too. It's still the best pizza I ever had. We didn't have a car until I was 4. It was an old black Dodge. I never had a telephone in my room. The only phone in the house was in the living room and it was on a party line. Before you could dial, you had to listen and make sure some people you didn't know weren't already using the line. Pizzas were not delivered to our home. But milk was. All newspapers were delivered by boys and all boys delivered newspapers. My brother delivered a newspaper, six days a week. It cost 7 cents a paper, of which he got to keep 2 cents. He had to get up at 6 am every morning. On Saturday, he had to collect the 42 cents from his customers. His favorite customers were the ones who gave him 50 cents and told him to keep the change. His least favorite customers were the ones who seemed to never be home on collection day. Movie stars kissed with their mouths shut. At least, they did in the movies. Touching someone else's tongue with yours was called French kissing and they didn't do that in the moves. French movies were dirty and we weren't allowed to see them. If you grew up in a generation before there was fast food, you may want to share some of these memories with your children and grandchildren. Just don't blame me if they bust a gut laughing. Growing up isn't what it uses to be, is it?

## MEMORIES From a Friend:

My Dad is cleaning out my grandmother's house (she dies in December) and he brought me an old Royal Crown Cola bottle. In the bottle top was a stopper with a bunch of holes in it. I knew immediately what it was, but my daughter had no idea. She thought they had tried to make a salt shaker or something. I knew it as the bottle that sat on the end of the ironing board to 'sprinkle' clothes with because we didn't have steam irons. Man I am old.

### How many do you remember?

Head lights dimmer switches on the floor.
Ignition switches on the dashboard.
Heaters mounted on the inside of the fire wall.
Real ice boxes.
Pant leg clips for bicycles without chain guards.
Soldering irons you heat on a gas burner.
Using hand signals for cars without turn signals.

### Older Than Dirt Quiz:

Count all the ones that you remember not the ones you were told about. Ratings at the bottom.
1. Blackjack Chewing Gum
2. Wax coke-shaped bottles with colored sugar water
3. Candy cigarettes
4. Soda pop machines that dispensed glass bottles
5. Coffee shops or diners with tableside juke boxes

6.  Home milk delivery in glass bottles with cardboard stoppers
7.  Party lines
8.  Newsreels before the movie
9.  P.F. Flyers
10. Butch wax
11. TV test patterns that came on at night after the last show and were there until TV shows started again in the morning (there were only 3 channels).
12. Peashooters
13. Howdy Doody
14. 45 RPM records
15. S & H Greenstamps
16. Hi-fi's
17. Metal ice trays with lever
18. Mimeograph paper
19. Blue flashbulb
20. Packards
21. Roller skate keys
22. Cork popguns
23. Drive-ins
24. Studebakers
25. Wash tub wringers
26. Lionel trains running under the Christmas tree
27. Dodge ball in the school yard

If you remembered 0-5 = You're still young.
If you remembered 6-10 = You're getting older
If you remembered 11-15 = Don't tell your age
If you remembered 16-25 = You're older than dirt!

I might be older than dirt but those memories are the best part of my life.

I dialed a number and got the following recording: "I am not available right now, but thank you for caring enough to call. I am making some changes in my life. Please leave a message after the beep. If I do not return your call, you are one of the changes."

Aspire to inspire before you expire.

My wife and I had words, but I didn't get to use mine.

Frustration is trying to find your glasses without your glasses.

Blessed are those who can give without remembering and take without forgetting.

The irony of life is that, by the time you're old enough to know your way around, you're not going anywhere.

God made man before woman so as to give him time to think of an answer for her first question.

I was always taught to respect my elders, but it keeps getting harder to find one.

Every morning is the dawn of a new error.
The quote of the month is by Jay Leno: "With hurricanes, tornadoes, fires out of control, mud slides, flooding, sever thunderstorms tearing up the country from one end to another, and with the threat of bird flu and terrorist attacks, "Are we sure this is a good time to take God out of the Pledge of Allegiance?"

A man was at the country club for his weekly round of golf. He began his round with an eagle on the first hole and a birdie on the second. On the third hole he had just scored his first ever hole-in-one when his cell phone rang. It was a doctor notifying him that his wife had just been in a terrible accident and was in critical condition and in the ICU. The man told the doctor to inform his wife where he was and that he'd be there as soon as possible. As he hung up he realized he as leaving what was shaping up to be his best round of golf. He decided to get in a couple of more holes before heading to the hospital. He ended up playing all eighteen, finishing his round shooting a personal best

61, shattering the club record by five strokes and beating his previous best game by more than 10. He was jubilant…then he remembered his wife. Feeling guilty he dashed to the hospital. He saw the doctor in the corridor and asked about his wife's condition. The doctor glared at him and shouted, "You went ahead and finished your round of golf didn't you! I hope you're proud of yourself! While you were out for the past four hours enjoying yourself at the country club your wife has been languishing in the ICU! It's just as well you went ahead and finished that round because it will be more that likely your last!" "For the rest of her life she will require 'round the clock' care. And you'll be her caregiver!" The man was feeling so guilty he broke down and sobbed. The doctor snickered and said, "Just fucking with you. She's dead. What'd you shoot?"

## Drops of Water

A lady goes to the bar on a cruise ship and orders a Scotch with two drops of water. As the bartender gives her the drink she says, "I'm on this cruise to celebrate my 80th birthday and it's today." The bartender says, "Well, since it's your birthday, I'll buy you a drink. In fact, this one is on me." As the woman finishes her drink, the woman to her right say, "I would like to buy you a drink, too." The old woman says, "Thank you. Bartender, I want a Scotch with two drops of water." "Coming up," says the bartender. As she finishes that drunk, the man to her left says, "I would like to buy you one, too." The old woman says, "Thank you. Bartender, I want another Scotch with two drops of water." "Coming right up," the bartender says. AS he gives her the drink, he says, "Ma'am, I'm dying of curiosity. Why the Scotch with only two drops of water?" The old woman replies, "Sonny, when you're my age, you've learned how to hold your liquor. Holding your water, however, is a whole other issue."

"OLD" IS WHEN… Your sweetie says, "let's go upstairs and make love," and you answer, "Pick one; I can't do both!"
"OLD" IS WHEN…Your friends compliment you on your new alligator shoes and you're barefoot.
"OLD" IS WHEN…A sexy baby catches your fancy and your

96

pacemaker opens the garage door.

"OLD IS WHEN…Going bra-less pulls all the wrinkles out of your face.

"OLD" IS WHEN…You don't care where your spouse goes, just as long as you don't have to go alone.

"OLD" IS WHEN…You are cautioned to slow down by the doctor instead of by the police.

"OLD" IS WHEN… 'Getting a little action' means you don't need to take any fiber today.

"OLD" IS WHEN…"Getting lucky" means you find your car in the parking lot.

"OLD" IS WHEN…An "all nighter" means not getting up to use the bathroom.

AND

"OLD"…IS WHEN You are not sure these are jokes?

There was a man who worked for the Post Office whose job was to process all the mail that had illegible addresses. One day, a letter came addressed in a shaky handwriting to God with no actual address. He thought he should open it to see what it was about. The letter read: Dear God, I am an 83 year old widow, living on a very small pension. Yesterday someone stole my purse. It had $100 in it, which was all the money I had until my next pension payment. Next Sunday is Christmas, and I had invited two of my friends over for dinner. Without that money, I have nothing to buy food with, have no family to turn to, and you are my only hope. Can you please help me? Sincerely, Edna The postal worker was touched. He showed the letter to all the other workers. Each one dug into his or her wallet and came up with a few dollars. By the time he made the rounds, he had collected $96, which they put into an envelope and sent to the woman. The rest of the day, all the workers felt a warm glow thinking of Edna and the dinner she would be able to share with her friends. Christmas came and went. A few days later, another letter came from the same old lady to God. All the workers gathered around while the letter was opened. It read: Dear God, How can I ever thank you enough for what you did for me? Because of your gift of love, I was able to fix a glorious dinner for my friends. We had a very nice day and I told my friends of your wonderful Gift. By the way, there was $4 missing. I think it might have been those Bastards at the post office. Sincerely, Edna

Some guy bought a new fridge for his house. To get rid of his old fridge, he put it in his front yard and hung a sign on it saying: 'Free to good home. You want it, you take it.' For three days the fridge sat there without even one person looking twice at it. He eventually decided that people were too un-trusting of this deal. It looked too good to be true, so he changed the sign to read: 'Fridge for sale $50." The next day someone stole it!

One day I was walking down the beach with some friends when someone shouted…"Look at that dead bird!" Someone looked up at the sky and said…"where?"

While looking at a house, my brother asked the estate agent which direction was north because, he explained, he didn't want the sun waking him up every morning. She asked, "Does the sun rise in the north?" When my brother explained that the sun rises in the east, and has for sometime, she shook her head and said, "Oh, I don't keep up with that stuff."

My colleague and I were eating our lunch in our cafeteria, when we overheard one of the administrative assistants talking about the sunburn she got on her weekend drive to the beach. She drove down in a convertible, but "didn't think she'd get sunburned because the car was moving."

My sister has a lifesaving tool in her car it's designed to cut through a seat belt if she gets trapped. She keeps it in the trunk.

I was hanging out with a friend when we saw a woman with a nose ring attached to an earring by a chain. My friend said, "Wouldn't the chain rip out every time she turned her head?" I had to explain that a person's nose and ear remain the same distance apart no matter which way the head is turned.

I couldn't find my luggage at the airport baggage area. So I went to the lost luggage office and told the woman there that my bags never showed up. She smiled and told me not to worry because she was a trained professional and I was in good hands. "Now," she asked me, "Has your plane arrived yet?"

While working at a pizza parlor I observed a man ordering a small pizza to go. He appeared to be alone and the cook asked him if he would like it cut into 4 pieces or 6. He thought about it for some time before responding. "Just cut it into 4 pieces; I don't think I'm hungry enough to eat 6 pieces.

## Garage Door

The boss walked into the office one morning not knowing his zipper was down and his fly area wide open. His assistant walked up to him and said, "This morning when you left your house, did you close your garage door?" The boss told her he knew he'd closed the garage door, and walked into his office puzzled by the question. As he finished his paperwork, he suddenly noticed his fly was open, and zipped it up. He then understood his assistant's question about his "garage door." He headed out for a cup of coffee and paused by her desk to ask, "When my garage door was open, did you see my Hummer parked in there?" She smiled and said, "No, I didn't. All I saw was an old minivan with two flat tires."

An elderly gentleman had serious hearing problems for a number of years. He went to the doctor and the doctor was able to have him fitted for a set of hearing aids that allowed the gentleman to hear 100%. The elderly gentleman went back in a month to the doctor and the doctor said, "Your hearing is perfect. Your family must be really pleased that you can hear again." The gentleman replied, "Oh, I haven't told my family yet. I just sit around and listen to the conversations. I've changed my will three times!"

A little old man shuffled slowly into an ice cream parlor and pulled himself slowly, painfully, up onto a stool. After catching his breath, he ordered a banana split. The waitress asked kindly, "Crushed nuts?" "No," he replied, "Arthritis."

Two elderly gentlemen from a retirement center were sitting on a bench under a tree when one turns to the other and says: "Slim, I'm 83 years old now and I'm just full of aches and pains. I know you're about my age. How do you feel?" Slim says, "I feel just like a newborn baby." "Really!? Like a newborn baby!?" "Yep. No hair, no teeth, and I think I just wet my pants."

An elderly couple had dinner at another couple's house, and after eating, the wives left the table and went into the kitchen. The two gentlemen were talking and one said, "Last night we went out to a new restaurant and it was really great. I would recommend it very highly." The other man said, "What is the name of the restaurant?" The first man thought and thought and finally said, "What is the name of that flower you give to someone you love? You know…The one that's red and has thorns." "Do you mean a rose?" "Yes, that's the one," replied the man. He then turned towards the kitchen and yelled, "Rose, what's the name of that restaurant we went to last night?"

Hospital regulations require a wheelchair for patients being discharged. However, while working as a student nurse, I found one elderly gentleman already dressed and sitting on the bed with a suitcase at his fee, who insisted he didn't need my help to leave the hospital. After a chat about rules being rules, he reluctantly let me wheel him to the elevator. On the way down I asked him if his wife was meeting him. "I don't know," he said. "She's still upstairs in the bathroom changing out of her hospital gown."

A couple in their nineties are both having problems remembering things. During a checkup, the doctor tells them that they're physically okay, but they might want to start writing things down to help them remember. Later that night, while watching TV, the old man gets up from his chair. "Want anything while I'm in the kitchen?" he asks. "Will you get me a bowl of ice cream?" "Sure." "Don't you think you should write it down so you can remember it?" she asks. "NO, I can remember it." "Well, I'd like some strawberries on top, too. Maybe you should write it down, so's not to forget it?" He says, "I can remember that. You want a bowl of ice cream with strawberries." "I'd also like whipped cream. I'm certain you"ll forget that , write it down?" she asks. Irritated, he says, "I don't need to write it down, I can remember it! Ice cream with strawberries and whip cream – I got it, for goodness sake!: Then he toddles into the kitchen. After about 20 minutes, the old man returns from the kitchen and hands his wife a plate of bacon and eggs. She stares at the plate for a moment. "Where's my toast?"

A senior citizen said to his eighty-year old buddy? "So I hear you're getting married?" "Yep!" "Do I know her?" "Nope!" "This woman, is she good looking?" "Not really." "Is she a good cook?" "Naw, she can't cook too well." "Does she have lots of money?" "Nope! Poor as a church mouse." "Well, then, is she good in bed?" "I don't know." "Why in the world do you want to marry her then?" "Because she can still drive!"

Three old guys are out walking. First one says, "Windy, isn't it?" Second one says, "No, it's Thursday!" Third one says, "So am I. Let's go get a beer."

A man was telling his neighbor, "I just bought a new hearing aid. It cost me four thousand dollars, but it's state of the art. It's perfect." "Really," answered the neighbor. "What kind is it?" "Twelve thirty."

Morris, an 82 year-old man, went to the doctor to get a physical. A few days later, the doctor saw Morris walking down the street with a gorgeous young woman on his arm. A couple of days later, the doctor spoke to Morris and said, "You're really doing great, aren't you?" Morris replied, "Just doing what you said, Doc, get a hot mamma and be cheerful." The doctor said, "I didn't say that. I said, "You've got a heart murmur; be careful."

After 30+ years of marriage, a couple were lying in bed one evening, when the wife felt her husband begin to fondle her in ways he hadn't in quite some time. It almost tickled as his fingers started at her neck, and then began moving down past the small of her back. He then caressed her shoulders and neck, slowly worked his hand down over her breast stopping just over her lower stomach. He ten proceeded to place his hand on her left inner arm, caressed past the side of her breast again, working down her side, passed gently over her buttock and down her leg to her calf. The, he proceeded up her inner thigh, stopping just at the uppermost portion of her leg. He continued in the same manner on the right side, then suddenly stopped. Rolled over and started to watch the tv. As she had become quite aroused by this caressing, she asked in a loving voice, "That was wonderful. Why did you stop?" He said, "I found the remote."

Attorney: "What was the first thing your husband said to you that morning?"
Witness: He said, "Where am I, Cathy?"
Attorney: "And why did that upset you?"
Witness: "My name is Susan!"

Attorney: "What gear were you in at the moment of the impact?"
Witness: "Gucci sweats and Reeboks."

Attorney: "Are you sexually active?"
Witness: "No, I just lie there."

Witness: "Because his brain was sitting on my desk in a jar."
Attorney: "I see, but could the patient have still been alive, nevertheless?"
Witness: "Yes, it is possible that he could have been alive and practicing law."

Attorney: "This myasthenia gravis, does it affect your memory at all?"
Witness: "Yes."
Attorney: "And in what ways does it affect your memory?"
Witness: "I forget."
Attorney: "You forget? Can you give us an example of something you forgot?"

Attorney: "Do you know if your daughter has ever been involved in voodoo?"
Witness: "We both do."
Attorney: "Voodoo?"
Witness: "We do."
Attorney" "You do?"
Witness: "Yes, voodoo."

Attorney: "Now, doctor, isn't it true that when a person dies in his sleep, he doesn't know about it until the next morning?"
Witness: Did you actually pass the bar exam?"

Attorney: "The youngest son, the twenty-year-old, how old is he?"
Witness: "He's twenty, much like your IQ."

Attorney: "Were you present when your picture was taken?"
Witness: "Are you shitting me?"

Attorney: "So the date of conception (of the baby) was August 8th?"
Witness: "Yes."
Attorney: "And what were you doing at that time?"
Witness: "Getting laid."

Attorney: "She had three children, right?"
Witness: "Yes."
Attorney: "How many were boys?"
Witness: "None."

Attorney: "Were there any girls?"
Witness: "Your Honor, I think I need a different attorney. Can I get a new attorney?"

Attorney: "How was your first marriage terminated?"
Witness: "By death."

Attorney: "And by whose death was it terminated?"
Witness: "Take a guess."

Attorney: "Can you describe the individual?"
Witness: "He was about medium height and had a beard."
Attorney: "Was this a male or a female?"
Witness: "Unless the circus was in town, I'm going with male."

Attorney: "Is your appearance here this morning pursuant to a deposition notice which I sent to your attorney?"
Witness: "No, this is how I dress when I go to work."

Attorney: "Doctor, how many of your autopsies have you performed on dead people?"
Witness: "All of them. The live ones put up too much of a fight."

Attorney: "All your reponses MUST be oral, OK? What school did you go to?"
Witness: "Oral."

Attorney: "Do you recall the time that you examined the body?"
Witness: "The autopsy started around 8:30 pm."
Attorney: "And Mr. Denton was dead at the time?"
Witness: "If not, he was by the time I finished."

Attorney: "Are you qualified to give a urine sample?"
Witness: "Are you qualified to ask that question?"

# MONTANA STATE TROOPER

In most of the United State there is a policy of checking on any stalled vehicle on the highway when temperatures drop to single digits or below. About 3 AM one very cold morning, Montana State Trooper Allan Nixon #658 responded to a call there was a car off the shoulder of the road outside Great Falls, Montana. He located the car, stuck in deep snow and with the engine still running. Pulling in behind the car with his emergency lights on, the trooper walked to the driver's door to find an older man passed out behind the wheel with a nearly empty vodka bottle on the seat beside him. The driver came awake when the trooper tapped on the window. Seeing the rotating lights in his rearview mirror, and the state trooper standing next to his car, the man panicked. He jerked the gearshift into drive and hit the gas. The car's speedometer was showing 20-30-40 and then 50 MPH, but it was still tuck in the snow, wheels spinning. Trooper Nixon, having a sense of humor, began running in place next to the speeding (but stationary) car. The driver was totally freaked, thinking the trooper was actually keeping up with him. This goes on for about 30 seconds, then the trooper yelled. "PULL OVER!" The man nodded, turned his wheel and stopped the engine. Needless to say, the man from North Dakota was arrested and is probably still shaking his head over the state trooper in Montana who could run 50 miles per hour.

## How to Treat a Woman

Wine her. Dine her. Call her. Hold her. Surprise her. Compliment her. Smile at her. Listen to her. Laugh with her. Cry with her. Romance her. Encourage her. Believe in her. Pray with her. Pray for her. Cuddle with her. Shop with her. Give her jewelry. Buy her flowers. Hold her hand. Write love letters to her. Go to the ends of the earth and back again for her.
How to Treat a Man
Show up naked. Bring chicken wings. Don't block the TV.

A woman was sitting at a bar enjoying an after work cocktail with her girlfriends when an exceptionally tall, handsome, extremely sexy, middle-aged man entered. He was so striking that the woman could not take her eyes off him. The young-at-heart man noticed her overly attentive stare and walked directly toward her (as all men will). Before she could offer her apologies for staring so rudely, he leaned over and whispered to her, "I'll do anything, absolutely anything that you want me to do, no matter how kinky, for $20.00….on one condition." Flabbergasted, the woman asked what the condition was. The man replied, "You have to tell me what you want me to do in just three words." The woman considered his proposition for a moment, and then slowly removed a $20 bill from her purse, which she pressed into the man's hand along with her address. She looked deeply into his eyes, and slowly and meaningfully said…"Clean my house."

Petra and Chela, two comadres, are talking. Petra: Ese senor George Garcia, asked me out for a date. I know you went out with him last week, and I wanted to talk with you about him before I give him my answer. Chela: Pues, le' me tell you sonting. He cho's up at my casa a las 7 and dressed good. Relly nice you know. And he brings me flawers and una caja de chocolates, mas suave! Then he takes me downstairs, and what's there but a beautiful car limousine, con chauffeur y toda la madre. Then he takes me out for dinner…mas bueno, el lobster. Then we go see a cho'…Let me tell you Petra, I enjoyed it so much I could hab died from pleachure! So then, we are coming back to my house, and he turns into an ANIMAL. Mas Loco que la chingada, he tears off my espensive new dress that I bought at Target and has his way with me…two times!" Petr: No la chingues! So, you telling me I shouldn't go out with him?" Chela: NO, PENDEJA!! I'm just saying, wear an old dress from Wal-Mart.

How the Fight Started

When I got home last night, my wife demanded that I take her some place expensive…so I took her to a gas station. And then the fight started.

I took my wife to a restaurant. The waiter, for some reason, took my order first. "I'll have the strip steak, medium rare, please." He said, "Aren't you worried about the mad cow/" "Nah, she can order for herself." And then the fight started.

A woman is standing nude, looking in the bedroom mirror. She is not happy with what she sees and says to her husband, "I feel horrible, I look old, fat and ugly. I really need you to pay me a compliment." The husband replies, "Your eyesight's darn near perfect." And then the fight started.

My wife and I are watching Who Wants To Be A Millionaire while we were in bed. I turned to her and said, "Do you want to have sex?" "No," she answered. I then said, "Is that your final answer?" She didn't even look at me this time, simply saying "Yes," So I said, "Then I'd like to phone a friend." And then the fight started.

After retiring, I went to the Social Security office to apply for Social Security. The woman behind the counter asked me for my driver's license to verify my age. I looked in my pockets and realized I had left my wallet at home. I told the woman that I was very sorry, but I would have to go home and come back later. The woman said, "Unbutton your shirt." So I opened my shirt revealing my curly silver hair. She said, "That silver hair on your chest is proof enough for me, and she processed my Social Security application. When I got home, I excitedly told my wife about my experience at the Social Security office. She said, "You should have dropped your pants. You might have gotten Disability too. And then the fight started.

Saturday morning I got up early, quietly dressed, made my lunch, grabbed the dog and slipped quietly into the garage. I hooked up the boat up to the truck, and proceeded to bak out into a torrential downpour. The wind was blowing 50 mph, so I pulled back into the garage, turned on the radio, and discovered that the weather would be bad all day. I went back into the house, quietly undressed and slipped back into bed. I cuddled up to my wife's back, now with a different anticipation, and whispered, "The weather out there is terrible. My loving wife of 10 years replied, "Can you believe my stupid husband is out fishing in that?" And that's how the fight started.

My wife and I were sitting at a table at my high school reunion, and I kep staring at a drunken lady swigging her drink as she sat alone at a nearby table. My wife asked, "Do you know her?" "Yes," I signed, "she's my old girlfriend. I understand she took to drinking right after we split up those many years ago, and I hear she hasn't been sober since. ""My God!" says my wife, "Who would think a person could go on celebrating that long?" And then the fight started.

I rear-ended a car this morning. So, there we were alongside the road and slowly the other driver got out of his car. You know how sometimes you just get soooo stressed and little things just seem funny? Yeah, well I couldn't believe it... He was a DWARF!!! He stormed over to my car, looked up at me, and shouted, "I AM NOT HAPPY!!!! So, I looked down at him and said, "Well, then which one are you?" And then the fight started.

Muldoon lived alone in the Irish countryside with only a pet dog for company. One day the dog died, and Muldoon went to the parish priest and asked, "Father, my dog is dead. Could ya' be saying a Mass for the poor creature?" Father Patrick replied, "I'm afraid not; we cannot have services for an animal in the church. But there are some Baptists down the land, and there's no tellin' what they believe. Maybe they'll do something for the creature." Muldoon said, "I'll go right away Father. Do ya think $5,000 is enough to donate to them for the service?" Father Patrick exclaimed, "Sweet Mary, Mother of Jesus! Why didn't ya tell me the dog was Catholic?"

An elderly man walks into a confessional. The following conversation ensues: Man: "I am 92 years old, have a wonderful wife of 70 years, many children, grandchildren and great grandchildren. Yesterday, I picked up two college girls hitchhiking. We went to a motel where I had sex with each of them three times." Priest: "Are you sorry for your sins?" Man: "What sins?" Priest: "What kind of a Catholic are you?" Man: "I'm Jewish." Priest: "Why are you telling me all this?" Man: "I'm 92 years old…I'm telling everybody."

A married Irishman went into the confessional and said to his priest, "I almost had an affair with another woman." The priest said, "What do you mean, almost?" The Irishman said, "Well, we got undressed and rubbed together, but then I stopped." The priest said, "Rubbing together is the same as putting it in. You're not to see that woman again. For your penance, say five Hail Mary's and put $50 in the poor box." The Irishman left the confessional, said his prayers and then walked over to the poor box. He paused for a moment and then started to leave. The priest, who was watching, quickly ran over to him saying, "I say that. You didn't put any money in that poor box!" The Irishman replied, "Yeah, but I rubbed the $50 on the box, and according to you, that's the same as putting it in!"

There once as a religious young woman who went to confession. Upon entering the confessional, she said, "Forgive me, Father, for I have sinned." The priest said, "Confess your sins and be forgiven." The young woman said, "Last night my boyfriend made mad passionate love to me seven times." The priest thought long and hard and then said, "Squeeze seven lemons into a glass and then drink the juice." The young woman asked, "Will this cleanse me of my sins?" The priest said, "No, but it will wipe that smile off of your face.'

Paddy had been drinking at his local Dublin pub all day and most of the night celebrating St. Patrick's Day. Mick, the bartender says, "You'll not be drinking anymore tonight, Paddy>" Paddy replied, "OK Mick, I'll bo on my way then." Paddy spins around on his stool and steps off. He falls flat on his face. "Darn," he says and pulls himself up by the stool and dusts himself off. He takes a step towards the door and falls flat on his face, "Darn, darn!" He looks to the doorway and thinks to himself that if he can just get to the door and some fresh air he'll be fine. He belly crawls to the door and shimmies up to the door frame. He sticks his head outside and takes a deep breath of fresh air, feels much better and takes a step out onto the sidewalk and falls flat on his face. "By jeepers....I'm a little crocked," he says. He can see his house just a few doors down, and crawls to the door, hauls himself up the door frame, opens the door and shimmies inside. He takes a look up the stairs to his bedroom door and says "I can make it to the bed." He takes a step into the room and falls flat on his face. He says, "Darn it" and falls into bed. The next morning, his wife, Jess, comes into the room carrying a cup of coffee and says, "Get up Paddy. Did you have a bit to drink last night?" Paddy says, "I did, Jess. I was really crocked. But how'd you know?" "Mick phoned and you left your wheelchair at the pub."

How many women with memopause does it take to change a light bulb? One! ONLY ONE!!!! And do you know WHY? Because no one else in this house knows HOW to change a light bulb! They don't even know that the bulb is BURNED OUT! They would sit in the dark for THREE DAYS before they figured it out. And, once they figured it out, they wouldn't be able to find the #&%!* light bulbs despite the fact they've been in the SAME CABINET for the past 17 YEARS! But if they did, by some miracle of God, actually find them, TWO DAYS LATER, the chair they dragged to stand on to change the STUPID light bulb would STILL BE IN THE SAME SPOTT!!!!! AND UNDERNEAT IT WOULD BE THE WRAPPER THE FREAKING LIGHT BULBS CAME IN!!! BECAUSE NO ONE EVER PICKS UP OR CARRIES OUT THE GARBAGE!!!!! IT'S A WONDER WE HAVEN'T ALL SUFFOCATED FROM THE PILES OF GARBAGE THAT ARE A FOOT DEEP THROUGHTOUT THE ENTIRE HOUSE!! IT WOULD TAKE AN ARMY TO CLEAN THIS PLACE! AND DON'T EVEN GET ME STARTED ON WHO CHANGES THE TOILET PAPER ROLL!! I'm sorry. What was the question?

## Tampons (A TRUE STORY)

Tampons to the rescue in Iraq!! Don't worry. It's from the mother of a Marine in Iraq. My son told me how wonderful the care packages we had sent them from the ladies auxillary were and wanted me to tell everyone thank you. He said that one guy we'll call Marine X got a female care package and everyone was giving him a hard time. My son said, "Marine X got some really nice smelling lotion and everyone really likes it, so every time he goes to sleep they steal it from him." I told my son I was really sorry about the mistake, and if he wanted I would send Marine X another package. He told me not to worry about Marine X because every time I send something to him, he shares it with Marine X. He said when my husband and I sent the last care package, Marine X came over to his cot picked up the box, started fishing through it and said, "What'd we get this time?" But my son said they had the most fun with Marine Xs package. He said he wasn't sure who it was supposed to go to, but the panties were size 20, and he said on of the guys got on top of the Humvee and jumped off with the panties over his head and yelled, "Look at me, I'm an Airborned Ranger!!!" One of the guys attached the panties to an antenna and it blew in the wind like a windsock. He said it entertained them for quite awhile. Then of course…they had those tampons. When he brought this up, my imagination just went running, but he continued. My son said they had to go on a mission and Marine X wanted the Chap-Stick and lotion for the trip. He grabbed a bunch of the items from his care package and got in the Humvee. As luck would have it he grabbed the tampons too, and my son said everyone was teasing him about "not forgetting the feminine hygiene products." He said things went well for a while, then the convoy was ambushed and a Marine was shot. He said the wound was pretty clean, but it was deep. He said they were administering first aid but couldn't get the bleeding to slow down, and someone said, "Hey! Use Marine X's tampons!" My son said they put the tampon in the wound. At this point my son profoundly told me, "Mom, did you know that tampons expand?" (Well…yeah?) They successfully slowed the bleeding until the guy got better medical attention. When they went to check on him later, the surgeon told them, "You guys saves his life. If you hadn's stopped that bleeding he would have bled to death." My son said, "Mom, the tampons sent by the Marine Moms by mistake save a Marine's life." At this point I asked him, "Well, what did you do with the rest of the tampons?" He said, "Oh, we divided them up and we all have them in our flak jackets, and I kept two for our first aid kit." I am absolutely amazed by the ingenuity of our Marines. I can't believe that something that started out as a mistake then turned into a joke, ended up saving someone's life. My sister said she doesn't believe in mistakes. She believes God had a plan all along. She believes that "female care package" was sent to Marine X so save our Marine.

## STORY #1

Many years ago, Al Capone virtually owned Chicago. Capone wasn't famous for anything heroic. He was notorious for enmeshing the windy city in everything from bootlegged booze and prostitution to murder. Capone had a lawyer nicknamed "East Eddie." He as Capone's for a good reason. Eddie was very good! In fact, Eddie's skill at legal maneuvering kept Big Al out of jail for a long time. To show his appreciation, Capone paid him very well. Not only was the money big, but also, Eddie got special dividends. For instance, he and his family occupied a fenced-in mansion, with live-in help and all of the conveniences of the day. The estate was so large that it filled and entire Chicago city block. Eddie lived that high life of the Chicago mob and gave little consideration to the atrocity that went on around him. Eddie did have one soft spot, however. He had a son that he loved dearly. Eddie saw to it that his young son had clothes, cars, and a good education. Nothing was withheld. Price was no object. And, despite his involvement with organized crime, Eddie even tried to teach him right from wrong. Eddie wanted his son to be a better man than he was. Yet, with all his wealth and influence, there were two things he couldn't give his son; he couldn't pass on a good name or a good example. One day, East Eddie reached a difficult decision. East Eddie wanted to rectify wrongs he had done. He decided he would go to the authorities and tell the truth about Al "Scarface" Capone, clean up his tarnished name, and offer his son some semblance of integrity. To do this, he would have to testify against the Mob, and he knew that the cost would be great. So he testified. Within the year, Easy Eddie's life ended in a blaze of gunfire on a lonely Chicago street. But in his eyes, he had given his son the greatest gift he had to offer, at the greatest price he could ever pay. Police removed from his pockets a rosary, a crucifix, a religious medallion and a poem clipped from a magazine. The poem read: The clock of life is wound but once, and no man has the power to tell just when the hands will stop at late or early hour. Now is the only time you own. Live, love, toil with a will. Place no faith in time. For the clock may soon be still.

## STORY #2

World Was II produced many heroes. One such man was Lieutenant Commander Butch O'Hare. He was a fighter pilot assigned to the aircraft carrier Lexington in the South Pacific. One day his entire squadron was sent on a mission. After he was airborne, he looked at his fuel gauge and realized that someone had forgotten to top off his fuel tank. He would not have enough fuel to complete his mission and get back to his ship. His flight leader told him to return to the carrier. Reluctantly, he dropped out of formation and headed back to the fleet. As he as returning to the mother ship he saw something that turned his blood cold: a squadron of Japanese aircraft was speeding its way toward the American fleet. The American fighters were gone on a sortie, and the fleet was all but defenseless. He couldn't reach his squadron and bring them back in time to save the fleet. Nor could he warn the fleet of the approaching danger. There was only one thing to do. He must somehow divert them from the fleet. Laying aside all thoughts of personal safety, he dove into the formation of Japanese planes. Wing-mounted 50 caliber's blazed as he charged in, attacking one surprised enemy plane and then another. Butch wove in and out of the now broken formation and fired at as many planes as possible until all his ammunition was finally spent. Undaunted, he continued the assault. He dove at the planes, trying to clip a wing or tail in hopes of damaging as many enemy planes as possible and rendering them until to fly. Finally, the exasperated Japanese squadron took off in another direction. Deeply relieved, Butch O'Hare and his tattered fighter limped back to the carrier. Upon arrival, he reported in and related the event surrounding his return. The film from the gun-camera mounted on his plane told the tale. It showed the extent of Butch's daring attempt to protect his fleet. He had, in fact, destroyed five enemy aircraft. This took place on February 20, 1942, and for that action Butch became the Navy's first Ace of W.W. II, and the first Naval Aviator to win the Congressional Medal of Honor. A year later Butch was killed in aerial combat at the age of 29. His home town would not allow the memory of this W.W. II hero to fade, and today, O'Hare Airport in Chicago is named in tribute to the courage of this great man. So, the next time you find yourself at O'Hare International, give some thought to visiting Butch's memorial displaying his statue and his Medal of Honor. It's located between terminals 1 and 2. SO WHAT DO THESE TWO STORIES HAVE TO DO WITH EACH OTHER? Butch O'Hare was East Eddies' son. (Pretty cool, huh?)

## CLAY BALLS

A man was exploring caves by the seashore. In one of the caves he found a canvas bag with a bunch of hardened clay balls. It was like someone had rolled clay balls and left them out in the sun to bake. They didn't look like much, but they intrigued the man, so he took the bag out of the cave with him. As he strolled along the beach, he would throw the clay balls one a time out into the ocean as far as he could. He thought little about it, until he dropped one of the clay balls and it cracked open on a rock. Inside was a beautiful, precious stone! Excited, the man started breaking open the remaining clay balls. Each contained a similar treasure. He found thousands of dollars worth of jewels in the 20 or so clay balls he had left. Then it struck him. He had been on the beach a long time. He had thrown maybe 50 or 60 of the clay balls with their hidden treasure into the ocean waves. Instead of thousands of dollars in treasure, he could have taken home tens of thousands, but he had just thrown it away! It's like that with people. We look at someone, maybe even ourselves, and we see the external clay vessel. It doesn't look like much from the outside. It isn't always beautiful or sparkling, so we discount it. We see that person as less important than someone more beautiful or stylish or well known or wealthy but we have not taken the time to find the treasure hidden inside that person. There is a treasure in each and every one of us. If we take the time to get to know that person, and if we ask God to show us that person the way He sees them, then the clay begins to peel away and the brilliant gem begins to shine forth. May we not come to the end of our lives and find out that we have thrown away a fortune in friendships because the gems were hidden in bits of clay. May we see the people in our world as God sees them. I am so blessed by the gems of friendship I have with each of you. Thank you for looking beyond my clay vessel.

### Who says men don't remember anniversaries!

A woman awaked during the night to find that her husband was not in bed. She puts on her robe and goes downstairs to look for him. She finds him sitting at the kitchen table with a hot coffee in front of him. He appears to be in deep thought, just staring at the wall. She watches as he wipes a tear from his eye and takes a sip of his coffee. "What's the matter, dear?" she whispers as she steps into the room, "Why are you down here at this time of night?" The husband looks up from his coffee, "I am just remembering when we first met 20years ago and started dating. You were only 16. Do you remember back then?" he asks solemnly. The wife is touched to tears thinking that her husband is so caring, so sensitive. "Yes, I do" she replies. The husband pauses. The words were not coming easily. "Do you remember when your father caught us in the back seat of my car?" "Yes, I remember," said the wife, lowering herself into a chair beside him. The husband continues. "Do you remember when he shoved the shotgun in my face and said, "Either you marry my daughter, or I will send you to jail for 20 years?" "I remember that, too" she replies softly. He wipes another tear from his cheek and says, "I would have gotten out today."

Q: I've heard that cardiovascular exercise can prolong life; is this true?
A: Your heart is only good for so many beats, and that's it...Don't waste them on exercise. Everything wears out eventually. Speeding up your heart will not make you live longer; that's like saying you can extend the life of your car by driving it faster. Want to live longer? Take a nap.

Q: Should I cut down on meat and eat more fruits and vegetables? A: You must grasp logistical efficiencies. What does a cow eat? Hay and corn. And what are these? Vegetables. So a steak is nothing more than an efficient mechanism of delivering vegetables to your system. Need grain? Eat chicken. Beef is also a good source of field grass (green leafy vegetable). And a pork chop can give you 100% of your recommended daily allowance of vegetable products.

Q: Should I reduce my alcohol intake? A: No, not at all. Wine is made from fruit. Brandy is distilled wine, that means they take the water out of the fruity bit so you get even more of the goodness that way. Beer is also made out of grain. Bottoms up!

Q: How can I calculate my body/fat ratio? A: Well, if you have a body and you have fat, your ratio is one to one. If you have two bodies your ratio is two to one, etc.

Q: What are some of the advantages of participating in a regular exercise program? A: Can't think of a single one, sorry. My philosophy is: No pain…good!

Q: Aren't fried foods bad for you? A: YOU'RE NOT LISTENING!!! Foods are fried these days in vegetable oil. IN fact, they're permeated in it. How could getting more vegetables be bad for you?

Q: Will sit-ups help prevent me from getting a little soft around the middle? A: Definitely not! When you exercise a muscle, it gets bigger. You should only be doing sit-ups if you want a bigger stomach.

Q: Is chocolate bad for me? A: Are you crazy? HELLO Cocoa beans! Another vegetable!!! It's the best feel-good food around!

Q: Is swimming good for your figure? A: If swimming is good for your figure, explain whales to me.

Q: Is getting in-shape important for my lifestyle? A: Hey! "Round" is a shape!

1. The Japanese eat very little fat and suffer fewer heart attacks than Americans.
2. The Mexicans eat a lot of fat and suffer fewer heart attacks than Americans.
3. The Chinese drink very little red wine and suffer fewer heart attacks than Americans.
4. The Italians drink a lot of red wine and suffer fewer heart attacks than Americans.
5. The Germans drink a lot of beers and eat lots of sausages and fats and suffer fewer heart attacks than Americans.

CONCLUSION: Eat and drink what you like. Speaking English is apparently what kills you.

WILL YOU Live to see 80? Here's something to think about. I recently picked a new primary care doctor. After two visits and exhaustive Lab test, he said I was doing "fairly well" for my age. (I just turned 66). He asked, "Do you smoke tobacco, or drink beer or wine?" "Oh no," I replied. "I'm not doing drugs, either!" Then he asked, "Do you eat rib-eye steaks and barbecued ribs? I said, "Not much…my former doctor said that all red meat is very unhealthy!" "Do you spend a lot of time in the sun, like playing golf, sailing, hiking or bicycling?" "No, I don't," I said. He asked, "Do you gamble, drive fast cars, or have a lot of sex?" "No," I said. He looked at me and said, "Then, why do you even give a shit?"

In honor of the mother of the octuplets, Denny's is offering a new breakfast meal: the Octo-slam, you get eight eggs, no sausage, and the guy next to you has to pay the bill.

A child was asked to write a book report on the entire Bible. This is amazing and brought tears of laughter to my eyes. I wonder how often we take for granted that children understand what we are teaching? Through the eyes of a child: the children's Bible in a Nutshell. In the beginning, which occurred near the star, there was nothing but God, darkness, and some gas. The Bible says, "The Lord thy God is one, but I think He must be a lot older than that." Anyway, God said, "Give me a light!" and someone did. Then God made the world. But they weren't embarrassed because mirrors hadn't been invented yet. Adam and Eve disobeyed God by eating one bad apple, so they were driven from the Gardne of Eden. Not sure what they were driven in through, because they didn't have cars. Adam and Eve had a son, Cain, who hated his brother as long as he was Abel. Pretty soon all of the early people died off, except for Methuselah, who lived to be like a million or something. One of the next important people was Noah, who was a good guy, but one of his kids was kind of a Ham. Noah built a large boat and put his family and some animals on it. He asked some other people to join him, but they said they would have to take a rain check. After Noah came Abraham, Isaac, and Jacob was more famous than his brother, Esau, because Esau sold Jacob his birthmark in exchange for some pot roast. Jacob had a son named Joseph who wore a really loud sports coat. Another important Bible guy is Moses, whose real name was Charlton Heston. Moses led the Israel Lights out of Egypt and away from the evil Pharaoh after God sent ten plagueson Pharaoh's people. These plagues included frogs, mice, lice, bowels, and no cable. God fed the Israel Lights every day with manicotti. Then he gave them his Top Ten Commandments. These include: don't lie, cheat, smoke, dance, or covet your neighbor's stuff. Oh yeah, I just thought of one more: Humor they father and thy mother. One of Moses' best helpers was Joshua who was the first Bible guy to use spies. Joshua fought the battle of Geritol and the fence fell over on the town. After Joshua came David. He got to be king by killing a giant with a slingshot. He had a son named Solomon who had about 300 wives and 500 porcupines. My teacher says he was wise, but that doesn't sound very wise to me. After Solomon there were a bunch of major league prophets. One of these was Jonah, who was swallowed by a big whale and then barfed up on the shore. There were also some minor league prophets, but I guess we don't have to worry about them. After the Old Testament came the New Testament. Jesus is the star of The New. He was born in Bethlehem in a barn. (I wish I had been born in a barn too, because my mom is always saying to me "Close the door! Were you born in a barn?" It would be nice to say, "As a matter of fact, I was.") During His life, Jesus had many arguments with sinners like the Pharisees and the Democrats. Jesus also had twelve opossums. The worst one was Judas Asparagus. Judas was so evil that they named a terrible vegetable after him. Jesus was a great man. He healed many leopards and even preached to some Germans on the Mount. But the Democrats and all those guys put Jesus on trial before Pontius the pilot. Pilot didn't stick up for Jesus. He just washed his hands instead. Anyways, Jesus died for our sins, then came back to life again. He went up to Heaven but will be back at the end of the Aluminum. His return is foretold in the book of Revolution.

I'm hopeful you find this a useful tool to help you enjoy your game that much more as you enjoy the great outdoors.

Chapter 1- How to Properly Line Up Your Fourth Putt.

Chapter 2 – How to Hit a Nike from the Rough, when you Hit a Titleist from the tee.

Chapter 3 – How to Avoid the Water When You Lie 8 in a bunker.

Chapter 4 – How to Get More Distance off the Shank.

Chapter 5 – When to Give the Ranger the Finger.

Chapter 6 – Using Your Shadow on the Greens to Maximize Earnings.

Chapter 7 – When to Implement Handicap Management.

Chapter 8 – Proper Excuses for Drinking Beer Before 9:00 a.m.

Chapter 9 – How to Rationalize a 6 Hour Round.

Chapter 10 – When Does a Divot Become Classified as Sod.

Chapter 11 – How to Find That Ball That Everyone Else Saw Go in the Water.

Chapter 12 – Why Your Spouse Doesn't Care That You Birdied the 5th.

Chapter 13 – Using Curse Words Creatively to Control Ball

Flight.

Chapter 14 – When to Let a Foursome Play Through Your Twosome.

Chapter 15 – How to Relax When You Are Hitting Five Off the Tee.

Chapter 16 – When to Suggest Major Swing Corrections to Your Opponent.

Chapter 17 – God and the Meaning of the Birdie-to-Bogey Three Putt.

Chapter 18 – When to Regrip Your Ball Retriever.

Chapter 19 – Throwing Your Clubs: An Effective Stress-Reduction Technique.

Chapter 20 – Can You Purchase a Better Golf Game?

Chapter 21 – Why Male Golfers Will Pay $5.00 a Beer from a Cart Girl and Give her a $3 Tip, But Will Balk at $4.50 at the 19th Hole and Stiff the Bartender.

Dear Ma and Pa, I am well. Hope you are. Tell Brother Walt and Brother Elmer the Marine Corps beats working for old man Larson by a mile. Tell them to join up quick before all of the places are filled. I was restless at first because you got to stay in bed till nearly 6 a.m. but I am getting so I like to sleep late. Tell Walt and Elmer all you do before breakfast is smooth your cot, and shine some thing. No hogs to slop, feed to pitch, mash to mix, wood to split, fire to lay. Practically nothing. Men got to shave but it is not so bad, there's warm water. Breakfast is strong on trimmings like fruit juice, cereal, eggs, bacon, etc. but kind of weak on chops, potatoes, ham, steak, fried eggplant, pie and other regular food, but tell Walt and Elmer you can always sit by the two city boys that live on coffee. Their food, plus yours, holds you until noon when you get fed again. It's no wonder these city boys can't walk much. We go on "route marches," which the platoon sergeant says are long walks to harden us. It he thinks so, it's not my place to tell him different. A "route march" is about as far as to our mailbox at home. Then the city guys get sore feet and we all ride back in trucks. The country is nice but awful flat. The sergeant is like a school teacher he nags a lot. The captain is like the school board. Majors and colonels just ride around and frown. They don't bother you none. This next will Walt and Elmer with laughing. I keep getting medals for shooting. I don't know why. The bulls-eye is near as big as a chipmunk head and don't move, and it ain't shooting at you like the Higgettt boys at home. All you got to do is lie there all comfortable and hit it. You don't even load your own cartridges. The come in boxes. Then we have what they call hand-to-hand combat training. You get to wrestle with them city boys. I have to be real careful though, they break real easy. It ain't like fighting with that ole bull at home. I'm about the best they got in this except for that Tug Jordan from over in Devils Lake. I only beat him once. He joined up the same time as me, but I'm only 5'6" and 130 pounds and he's 6'8" and near 300 pounds dry. Be sure to tell Walt and Elmer to hurry and join before other fellers get onto this setup and come stampeding in. Your loving daughter, Darlene

A middle aged Chicana had a heart attack and was taken to the hospital. While on the operating table, she had a near death experience and the Creator appeared before her. Seeing the Creator, she asked, "Dios mio, is my time up?" Dios said, "No mijita, you have another 43 years, two months and eight days to live." The Chicana decided to stay in the hospital and have "the works" done: face-lift, liposuction, chi-chi lift, nalga lift and pansa tuck. She was all excited because she knew she had a long life ahead and wanted to look bien chingona! After her final operation, she was released from the hospital. While crossing the street on her way to a taqueria, she was hit and killed by a bus. Arriving in front of the Creator, she demanded, "Orale pues… que paso? I though you said I had another 40 years to go? Why didn't you pull me out of the path of the pinche bus?" The Creator replied, "Orale loca, I didn't recognize you!"

Mother was trying to get into America legally through Immigration. The Immigration Officer said, "Mujibar, you have passed all the tests, except there is one more test. Unless you pass it you cannot enter America." Mujibar said, "I am ready now sir for taking you testing."

The officer said, "Make a sentence using the words Yellow, Pink and Green." Mujibar thought for a few minutes and said, "Mister Officer, I am ready." The Officer said, "Go ahead." Mujibar said, "The telephone goes green, green, green, and I pink it up and say, yellow, this is Mujibar." Mujibar now lives in a neighborhood near you, and works at SBC on the Help Desk for your DSL service.

I was driving home from a meeting this evening about 5, stuck in traffic on Colorado Blvd. and the car started to choke and splutter and die. I barely managed to coast, cursing into a gas station, glad only that I would not be blocking traffic and would have a somewhat warm spot to wait for the tow truck. It wouldn't even turn over. Before I could make the call, I saw a woman walking out of the "quickie mart" building, and it looked like she slipped on some ice and fell into a Gas pump, so I got out to see is she was okay. When I got there, it looked like she had been overcome by sobs than that she had fallen; she was a young woman who looked really haggard with dark circles under her eyes. She dripped something as I helped her up and I picked it up to give it to her. It was a nickel. At that moment, everything came into focus for me; the crying woman, the ancient Suburban crammed full of stuff with 3 kids in the back (one in a car seat), and the gas pump reading $4.95. I asked her if she was okay and if she needed help, and she just kept saying "don't want my kids to see my crying," so we stook on the other side of the pump from her car. She said she was driving to California and that things were very hard for her right now. So I asked, "And you were praying?" That made her back away from me a little, but I assured her I was not a crazy person and said, "He heard you, and He sent me." I took out my card and swiped it through the card reader on the pump so she could fill up her car completely, and while it was fueling, walked to the next door McDonald's and bought 2 big bags of food, some gift certificates for more, and a big cup of coffee. She gave the food to the kids in the car, who attacked it like wolves, and we stood by the pump eating fried and talking a little. She told me her name and that she lived in Kansas City. Her boyfriend left two months ago and she had not been able to make ends meet. She knew she wouldn't have money to pay rent Jan. 1, and finally in desperation had finally called her parents, with whom she had not spoken in about 5 years. They lived in California and said she could come live with them and try to get on her feet there. So she packed up everything she owned in the car. She told the kids they were going to California for Christmas, but not that they were going to live there. I gave her my gloves, a little hug and said a quick prayer with her for safety on the road. As I was waling over to my car, she said, "So, are you like and angel or something?" This definitely made me cry. I said, "Sweetie, at this time of year angels are really busy, so sometimes God uses regular people." It was so incredible to be a part of someone else's miracle. And of course, you guessed it, when I got in my car it started right away and got me home with no problem. I'll put it in the shop tomorrow to check, but I suspect the mechanic won't find anything wrong.

## GOT TO LOVE EM – TENNESSEE

A guy from Tennessee passed away and left his entire estate to his beloved widow, but she can't touch it 'til she's 14.

How do you know when you're staying in a Tennessee hotel? When you call the front desk and say, "I gotta leak in my sink," and the clerk replies, "Go ahead."

How can you tell if a Tennessee redneck is married? There's dried tobacco juice on both sides of his pickup truck.

Did you hear that they have raised the minimum drinking age in Tennessee to 32? It seems they want to keep alcohol out of the high schools.

What do they call reruns of "Hee Haw" in Tennessee?
Documentaries.

Where was the toothbrush invented? Tennessee. If it had been invented anywhere else, it would have been called a teethbrush.

A Tennessee State trooper pulls over a pickup on I-64 and says to the driver, "Gotany I.D.?" and the driver replies "Boutwut?"

Did you hear about the $3 million Tennessee State Lottery? The winner gets $3.00 a year for a million years.

The Governor's mansion in Tennessee burned down! Yep. Pert' near took out the whole trailer park. The library was a total loss, too. Both books-POOF – up in flames and he hadn't even finished coloring one of them.

A new law was recently passed in Tennessee. When a couple gets divorced, they are STILL cousins.

A guy walks into a bar in Tennessee and orders a mudslide. The bartender looks at the man and says, "You ain't from 'round here are ya?" "No," replies the man, "I'm from Pennsylvania." The bartender looks at him and says, "Well, what do ya do in Pennsylvania?" "I'm a taxidermist," said the man. The bartender, looking very bewildered now, asks, "What in the world is a tax-e-derm-ist?" The man says, "I mount animals." The bartender stands back and hollers to the whole bar…"It's okay boys, he's one of us!"

I was thinking about how a status symbol of today is those cell phones that everyone has clipped on. I can't afford one. So, I'm wearing my garage door opener.

You know, I spent a fortune on deodorant before I realized that people didn't like me anyway.

I was thinking about old age and decided that it is "when you still have something on the ball, but yu are just too tired to bounce it."

I thought about making a fitness movie, for folks my age, and call it "Pumping Rust."

I have gotten that dreaded furniture disease. That's when your chest is falling into your drawers!

I know, when people see a cat's litter box, they always say, "Oh, have you got a cat?" Just once I want to say, "No, it's for company!"

Employment application blanks always ask "who is to be notified in case of an emergency." I think you should write, "A Good Doctor!"

Why do they put pictures of criminals up in the Post Office? What are we supposed to do, write to these men? Why don't they just put their pictures on the postage stamps so the mailmen could look for them while they deliver the mail? Or better yet, arrest them while they are taking their pictures!

I was thinking about how people seem to read the Bible a whole lot more as they get older. Then, it dawn on me, they were cramming for their finals. As for me, I'm just hoping God grades on the curve.

## CHECKING ACCOUNT

A crusty old man walks into a bank and says to the woman at the teller window. "I want to open a damn checking account." The astonished woman replies, "I beg your pardon, sir. I must have misunderstood you. What did you say?" "Listen up, dammit. I said I want to open a damn checking account, right now!" "I'm very sorry sir, but that kind of language is not tolerated in this bank." She replies. The teller leaves the window and goes over to the bank manager to inform him of the situation. The manager agrees that the teller does not have to listen to that kind of foul language. They both return to the window and the manager asks the old geezer, "Sir, what seems to be the problem here?" "There is no damn problem," the man says. "I just won $50 million bucks in the damn lottery and I want to open a damn checking account in this damn bank." "I see," says the manager, "and this bitch is giving you a hard time?"

A woman shopped for these items: a carton of eggs, a head of romaine lettuce, a 2 pound can of coffee, and a 1 pound package of bacon. As she was unloading her items on the conveyor belt to check out, a drunk standing behind her watched as she placed the items in front of the cashier. While the cashier was ringing up her purchases, the drunk calmly state, "You must be single." The woman was a bit startled by this proclamation, but she was intrigued by the derelict's intuition, since she was indeed single. She looked at her six items on the belt and saw nothing particularly unusual about her selections that could have tipped off the drunk to her marital status. Curiosity getting the better of her, she said "Well, you know what, you're absolutely correct. But how on earth did you know that?" The drunk replied, "Cause you're ugly."

If someone comes to your front door saying they are conducting a survey on deer ticks and asks you to take your clothes off and dance around with your arms up, DO NOT DO IT!! IT IS A SCAM; they only want to see you naked! I wish I'd gotten this yesterday. I feel so stupid now.

## The Collection Plate

Every Sunday, a little old lady placed $1,000 in the collection plate. This went on for weeks until the pastor, overcome by curiosity, approached her. "Ma'am, I couldn't help but notice that you put $1,000 a week in the collection plate," he stated. "Why yes", she replied, "every week my son sends me money, and what I don't need I give to the church." The pastor replied, "That's wonderful, how much does he send you?" The old lady said, "Oh, $20,000 a week." The pastor was amazed. "Your son is very successful, what does he do for a living?" "He's a veterinarian," she answered. "That is a very honorable profession," the pastor says. "Where does he practice?" The old lady says proudly, "Well, he has two cat houses in Las Vegas and one in Reno."

Dear Son, I am writing this slow 'cause I know you can't read fast. Three of your friends went off the bridge in a pickup truck. One was driving' and the other two were in the back. The driver rolled down the window and gout out. The other two drowned. They couldn't get the tailgate open. We don't live where we did when you left. Your dad read in the paper that most accidents happen within 20 miles of home, so we moved. I can't send you our address because the family that lived here before took the house numbers with them for their next house, so they wouldn't have to change their address. This place has a washer machine, but I don't use it. I put four socks in it, pulled the chain, and they disappeared. It only rained twice this week, three days the first time and four days the second time. We got a bill from the funeral home. They said if we don't make the last payment on Grandma's funeral, up she comes. Your Dad has a good, new job. He has 500 men under him. He is cutting grass at the cemetery. Your Uncle John fell in the whiskey vat. Some men tried to pull him out, but he fought them off and drowned. We cremated him. He burned for three days. Love, Mom P.S. We were gonna send you some money but we had already mailed this letter. Mom & Dad

A small Texas Wild Animal Park acquired a very rare species of gorilla. Within a few weeks, the gorilla, which was a female, because very difficult to handle. Upon examination, the park veterinarian determined the problem. The gorilla was in heat. To make matters worse, there was no male gorilla available. Reflecting on their problem, the park administrator thought of Bubba, redneck part-time intern, who was responsible for cleaning the animal's cages. Bubba, like most rednecks, had little sense, but possessed ample ability to satisfy a female of any species, approached with a proposition. Would he be willing to mate with the gorilla for $500.00? Bubba showed some interest, but said he would have to think the matter over carefully. The following day, Bubba announced that he would accept their offer, but only under the following four conditions: 1. "First," Bubba said, "I don't want to have to kiss her on the lips." The park administrator quickly agreed to this condition. 2. "Second," Bubba said, "you must never tell anyone about this." The part administrator again readily agreed to this condition. 3. "Third." Bubba said, "I want all the offspring to be raised Southern Baptist." Once again the administrator agreed. 4. And last of all Bubba stated, "You've got to give me another week to come up with the $500.00."

A man went to church one day and afterward he stopped to shake the preacher's hand. He said "Preacher, I'll tell you, that was a damned fine sermon. Damned good!" The preacher said, "Thank you sir, but I'd rather you didn't use profanity." The man said, "I was so damned impressed with that sermon I put five thousand dollars in the offering plate!" The preacher said, "No shit!"

Brenda and Steve took their six year old son to the doctor. With some hesitation, they explained that although their angel appeared to be in good health, they were concerned about his rather small penis. After examining the child, the doctor confidently declared, "Just feed him pancakes. That should solve the problem." The next morning when the boy arrived at breakfast, there was a large stack of warm pancakes in the middle of the table. "Gee, Mom," he exclaimed, "For me?" "Just take two," Brenda replied. "The rest are for your father."

There were two old men sitting on a park bench passing the day away talking. One old man asked the other, "How is your wife?" The second old guy replied, "I think she may be dead!" The first man asked, "What do you mean you THINK she is dead?" The second explained, "Well, the sex is the same but the dishes are starting to pile up."

An elderly couple was sitting around one evening and the man says to his wife, "Marsha, we are about to celebrate our 60$^{th}$ wedding anniversary. We've had a wonderful life together, full of contentment and blessings. But there's something I've always wondered about. Tell me the truth. Have you ever been unfaithful to me?" She hesitated a moment, then said, "Yes, Sidney, three times." "Three times? How could that happened?" Sidney asks. Marsha replied, "Well, do you remember right after we were married and we were so broke that the bank was about to foreclose on our little house?" "Yes, dear, those were really difficult times," replied Sidney. "And remember when I went to see the banker one night, and the next day the bank extended our loan?" "Gosh, that's really hard to take," said Sidney. "But since things were so bad at the time, I guess I can forgive you. What was the second time?" "Well," Marsha continued, "do you remember years later when you almost died of that heart problem because we couldn't afford an operation?" "Yes, of course," said Sidney. "Then you will remember that right after I went to see the doctor, he performed the operation at no cost?" "Yes, I remember," said Sidney, "and as much as that shocks me, I do understand that you did what you did out of love for me, so I forgive you. So, what was the third time?"

Marsha lowered her head and said, "Do you remember when you ran for president of your golf club and you needed 62 more votes?"

A plane leaves Los Angeles airport under the control of a Jewish captain. His copilot is Chinese. It's the first time they've flown together and an awkward silence between the two seems to indicate a mutual dislike. Once they reach cruising altitude, the Jewish captain activate the auto pilot, leans back in his seat, and mutters, "I don't like Chinese." "No ride Chinese?" asks the copilot, "why not?" "You people bombed Pearl Harbor, that's why!" "No, no," the copilot protests, "Chinese not bomb Pearhl Hahbah! That Japanese, not Chinese." "Japanese, Chinese, Vietnamese...doesn't matter, you're all alike!" There's a few minutes of silence. "No rike Jews!" the copilot suddenly announces. "Why not?" asks the captain. "Jews sink Titanic," the copilot responds. "Jews didn't sink the Titanic!" exclaims the captain, "It was an iceberg!" "Iceberg, Goldberg, Greenberg, Rosenberg, no mattah...all same!"

On the first day God created the dog. God said, "Sit all day by the door of your house and bark at anyone who comes in or walks past. I will give you a life span of twenty years." The dog said, "That's too long to be barking. Give me ten years and I'll give you back the other ten." So God agreed.

On the second day God created the monkey. God said, "Entertain people, do monkey tricks, make them laugh. I'll give you a twenty year life span." The monkey said, "How boring, monkey tricks for twenty years? I don't think so. Dog gave you back ten, so that's what I'll do too, okay?" And God agreed.

On the third day God created the cow. God said, "You must go to the field with the farmer all day long and suffer under the sun, have calves and give milk to support the farmer. I will give you a life span of sixty years." The cow said, "That's kind of a tough life you want me to live for sixty years. Let me have twenty and I'll give back the other forty." And God agreed again.

On the fourth day God created man. God said, "Eat, sleep, play, marry and enjoy your life. I'll give you twenty years." Man said, "What? Only twenty years! Tell you what, I'll take my twenty, and the forty the cow gave back and the ten the monkey gave back and the ten the dog gave back, that makes eighty, okay?" "Okay," said God, "You've got a deal."

So that is why the first twenty years we eat, sleep, play and enjoy ourselves: for the next forty years we slave in the sun to support our family; for the next ten years we do monkey tricks to entertain the grandchildren; and for the last ten years we sit on the front porch and bark at everyone. Life has now been explained to you.


The Year 1904

What a difference a century makes!
The average life expectancy in the U.S. was 47 years.
Only 14 percent of the homes in the U.S. had a bathtub.
Only 8 percent of the homes had a telephone.
A three minute call from Denver to New York City cost eleven dollars.
There were only 8,000 cars in the U.S., and only 144 miles of paved roads.
The maximum speed limit in most cities was 10 mph.
Alabama, Mississippi, Iowa, and Tennessee were each more heavily populated than California.
With a mere 1.4 million residents, California was only the 21st most populous state in the Union.
The tallest structure in the world was the Eiffel Tower!
Only 6 percent of all Americans had graduated high school.
Marijuana, heroin, and morphine were all available over the counter at corner drugstores.
According to one pharmacist, "Heroin clears the complexion, gives buoyancy to the mind, regulates the stomach and bowels and is, in fact, a perfect guardian oh health." (Shocking)

Eighteen percent of households in the U.S. had at least one full time servant or domestic.

There were only about 230 reported murders in the entire U.S.

Try to imagine what it may be like in another 100 years.

The average wage in the U.S. was 22 cents an hour.

The average U.S. worker made between $200 and $400 per year.

A competent accountant could expect to earn $2000 per year, a dentist $2,500 per year, a veterinarian between $1,500 and $4,000 per year and a mechanical engineer about $5,000 per year.

More than 95 percent of all births in the U.S. took place at home.

Ninety percent of all U.S. physicians had no college education. Instead they attended medical schools, many of which were condemned in the press and by the government as "substandard."

Sugar cost four cents a pound.

Eggs were fourteen cents a dozen.

Coffee was fifteen cents a pound.

Most women only washed their hair once a month, and used borax or egg yolks for shampoo.

Canada passed a law prohibiting poor people from entering the country for any reason.

The five leading causes of death in the U.S. were:

1. Pneumonia and influenza
2. Tuberculosis
3. Diarrhea
4. Heart disease
5. Stroke

The American flag had 45 stars. Arizona, Oklahoma, New Mexico, and Alaska hadn't been admitted to the Union yet.

The population of Las Vegas, Nevada, was 30!!!

Crossword puzzles, canned beer, and iced tea hadn't been invented.

There was no Mother's Day or Father's Day.

Two of 10 U.S. adults couldn't read or write.

## Worst First Date

This was on the Tonight Show with Jay Leno. Jay went into the audience to find the most embarrassing first date that a woman ever had. The winner described her worst first date experience. There was absolutely no question as to why her tale took the prize! She said it was midwinter, snowing and quite cold and the guy had taken her skiing to Lake Arrowhead. It was a day trip (no overnight). They were strangers, after all, and truly had never met before. The outing was fun but relatively uneventful until they were headed home late that afternoon. They were driving back down the mountain, when she gradually began to realize that she should not have had that extra latte. They were about an hour away from anywhere with a restroom and the middle of nowhere! Her companion suggested she try to hold it, which she did for a while. Unfortunately, because of the heavy snow and slow going, there came a point where she told him that he had better stop and let her pee beside the road, or it would be the front seat of his car. They stopped and she quickly crawled out beside the car, yanked her pants down and started. Unfortunately, in the deep snow she didn't have good footing, so leaned her butt to rest against the rear fender to steady herself. Her companion stood on the side of the car watching for traffic and indeed was a real gentleman and refrained from peeking. All she could think about was the relief she felt despite the rather embarrassing nature of the situation. Upon finishing however, she soon became aware of another sensation. As she bent to pull up her pants the young lady discovered her buttocks were firmly glued against the car's fender. Thoughts of tongues frozen to pump handles immediately came to mind as she attempted to disengage her flesh from the icy metal. It was quickly apparent that she had a brand new problem due to the extreme cold. Horrified by her plight and yet aware of the humor she answered her date's concerns about what is taking so long with a reply that indeed, she was freezing her butt off and in need of some assistance. He came around the car as she tried to cover herself with her sweater and then, as she looked imploringly into his eyes, he burst out laughing. She too, got the giggles and when they finally managed to compost themselves, they assessed her dilemma. Obviously, as hysterical as the situation was, they also were faced with a real problem. Both agreed it would take something hot to free her chilly cheeks from the grip of the icy metal! Thinking about what had gotten here into the predicament in the first place, both quickly realized that there was only one way to get her free. So, as she looked the other way, her first time date proceeded to unzip his pants and pee her butt off the fender. As for the Tonight Show, she took the prize hands down...or perhaps that should be pants down. This gives a whole new meaning to being pissed off.

At 85 years of age, Morris married Lou Anne, a lovely 25 year old. Since her new husband is so old, Lou Anne decided that after their wedding she and Morris should have separate bedrooms, because she is concerned that her new, but aged husband may overexert himself it they spend the entire night together. After the wedding festivities Lou Anne prepares herself for bed and the expected "knock" on the door. Sure enough, the knock comes; the door opens and there is Morris, her 85 year old groom, ready for "action." They "unite as one." All goes well; Morris takes leave of his bride, and she prepares to go to sleep. After a few minutes, Lou Anne hears another knock on her bedroom door and it's Morris. Again, he is ready for "action." Somewhat surprised, but nonetheless willing, Lou Anne consents to more "conjugal bliss." When the lovebirds are done, Morris kissed his bride, bids her a fond goodnight and leaves. She is set to go to sleep again, but Morris is back again, rapping on the door, as fresh as a 25 year old, ready for more passion. Once again, they enjoy one another. But as Morris prepares to leave again, his young bride says to him, "I am thoroughly impressed that at your age you can perform so well and so often. I have been with guys less that a third of your age who were only good once. You are truly a great love, Morris." Morris, somewhat embarrassed, turns to Lou Anne and says, "You mean I was here already?"

<u>You're an EXTREME redneck if...</u>

You let your 14 year old daughter smoke at the dinner table in front of her kids.

The Blue Book value of your truck goes up and down depending on how much gas is in it.

You've been married three times and still have the same in-laws.

You think a woman who is "out of your league" bowls on a different night.

You need one more hole punched in your card to get a freebie at the House of Tattoos.

You can't get married to your sweetheart because there's a law against it.

You think loading the dishwasher means getting your wife drunk.

You wonder how service stations keep their restroom so clean.

Someone in your family died right after saying, "Hey, guys, watch this!"

You think Dom Perignon is a Mafia leader.

Your wife's hairdo was once ruined by a ceiling fan.

Your junior prom offered day care.

You think the last words of the "Star-Spangled Banner" are "Gentlemen, start your engines."

You lit a match in the bathroom and your house exploded right off its wheels.

The Halloween pumpkin on your porch has more teeth than your spouse.

You have to go outside to get something from the fridge.

One of your kids was born on a pool table.

A married man left work early one Friday afternoon. Instead of going home, however, he spent the weekend (and his money) partying with the boys. When he finally returned home on Sunday night, his wife really got on his case and stayed on it. After a couple of hours of swearing and screaming, his wife paused and pointed at him and made him an offer. "How would you like it if you didn't see me for a couple of days? The husband couldn't believe his luck, so he looked up, smiled and said, "That would suit me just fine!!" Monday went by, and the man didn't see his wife. Tuesday and Wednesday went by and he still didn't see her. Come Thursday, the swelling went down a bit and he could see her a little just out of the corner of his left eye.

Kurt was going out with a nice girl and finally popped the question. "Will you marry me, darling?" he asked. Lisa smiled coyly and said,

"Yes, if you'll buy me a mink." Kurt thought for a moment and then replied, "Okay, it's a deal, on one condition." "What is that?" Lisa asked. "You'll have to clean the cage," Kurt replied.

We've all heard about people having guts or balls. But do you really know the difference between them? In an effort to keep you informed, the definition for each is listed below…

GUTS – is arriving home late after a night out with the guys, being met by your wife with a broom, and having the guts to ask, "Are you still cleaning, or are you flying somewhere?"

BALLS – is coming home late after a night out with the guys, smelling of perfume and beer, lipstick on your collar, slapping your wife on the butt and having the balls to say: "You're next."

I hope this clears up any confusion on the definitions. Medically speaking, there is no difference in the outcome since both ultimately result in a extremely painful death.

## Two Women in Heaven

1st woman: HI! My name is Sandra.

2nd woman: Hi! I'm Sylvia. How'd you die?

1st woman: I froze to death.

2nd woman: How horrible!

1st woman: It wasn't so bad. After I quit shaking from the cold, I began to get warm and sleepy, and finally died a peaceful death. What about you?

2nd woman: I died of a massive heart attack. I suspected that my husband was cheating, so I came home early to catch him in the act. But instead, I found him all by himself in the den watching TV.

1st woman: So, what happened?

2nd woman: I was so sure there was another woman there somewhere that I started running all over the house looking. I ran up into the attic and searched, and down into the basement. Then I went through every closet and checked under all the beds. I kept this up until I had looked everywhere, and finally I became so exhausted that I just keeled over with a heart attck and died.

1st woman: Too bad you didn't look in the freezer---we'd both still

be alive.
PRICELESS!

A man realized he needed to purchase a hearing air, but he felt unwilling to spend much money. "How much do they run?" he asked the clerk. "That depends," said the salesman. "They run from $2.00 to $2,000." "Let's see the $2.00 model," he said. The clerk put the device around the man's neck. "You just stick this button in your ear and run this little string down to you pocket," he instructed. "How does it work?" the customer asked. "For $2.00 it doesn't work," the salesman replied. "But when people see it on you, they'll talk louder!"

Yesterday I was buying 2 large bags of Purina dog chow at Wal-Mart, for my dogs, Winston, Chief, Buckwheat and Toby. I was about to check out when a woman behind me asked if I had a dog. What did she think that I had an elephant? Since I had little else to do, on impulse, I told her that no, I didn't have a dog, and that I was starting the Purina Diet again although I probably shouldn't because I ended up in the hospital last time. On the bright side though, I'd lost 50 pounds before I awakened in an intensive care ward with tubes coming out of every hole in my body and IVs in both arms. I told her that it was essentially a perfect diet and that the way that it works is to load your pockets with Purina nuggets and simply eat one or two every time you feel hungry and that the food is nutritionally complete so I was going to try it again. I have to mention here that practically everyone in the line was enthralled with my story by now. Horrified, she asked if I ended up in intensive care because the dog food had poisoned me. I told her no; I had stopped in the middle of the parking lot to lick my butt and a car hit me. I thought the guy behind her was going to have a heart attack, he was laughing so hard! WAL-MART won't let me shop there anymore.

### Children in Church

A little boy was in a relative's wedding.
As he was coming down the aisle, he would take two steps,

stop, and turn to the crowd.
While facing the crowd, he would put his
hands up like claws and roar.
So it went, step, step, ROAR, step, step,
ROAR, all the way down the aisle.
As you can imagine, the crowd was near
tears from laughing so hard
by the time he reached the pulpit.
When asked what he was doing, the child sniffed and said,
"I was being the Ring Bear."
One Sunday in a Midwest City ,
a young child was "acting up" during the morning worship hour.
The parents did their best to maintain
some sense of order in the pew
but were losing the battle.
Finally, the father picked the little fellow up
and walked sternly up the aisle on his way out.
Just before reaching the safety of the foyer,
the little one called loudly to the congregation,
"Pray for me! Pray for me!"
One particular four-year old prayed,
"And forgive us our trash baskets
as we forgive those who put trash in our baskets."
A little boy was overheard praying:
"Lord, if you can't make me a better boy, don't worry about it.
I'm having a real good time like I am."
A Sunday School teacher asked her little children,
as they were on the way to church service,
"And why is it necessary to be quiet in church?"
One bright little girl replied, "Because people are sleeping."
A little boy opened the big and old family Bible with fascination,
looking at the old pages as he turned them.
Then something fell out of the Bible.
He picked it up and looked at it closely.
It was an old leaf from a tree that has been
pressed in between the pages.

"Mama, look what I found," the boy called out.
"What have you got there, dear?" his mother asked.
With astonishment in the young boy's voice he answered,
"It's Adam's suit".
The preacher was wired for sound with a lapel mike,
and as he preached, he moved briskly about the platform,
jerking the mike cord as he went.
Then he moved to one side,
getting wound up in the cord and nearly
tripping before jerking it again.
After several circles and jerks,
a little girl in the third pew leaned toward
her mother and whispered,
"If he gets loose, will he hurt us?"
Six-year old Angie , and her four-year old brother,
Joel , were sitting together in church.
Joel giggled, sang and talked out loud.
Finally, his big sister had had enough.
"You're not supposed to talk out loud in church."
"Why? Who's going to stop me?" Joel asked.
Angie pointed to the back of the church and said,
"See those two men standing by the door?
They're hushers."
My grandson was visiting one day when he asked ,
"Grandma, do you know how you and God are alike?"
I mentally polished my halo, while I asked,
"No, how are we alike?"
"You're both old," he replied.
A ten-year old, under the tutelage of her grandmother,
was becoming quite knowledgeable about the Bible.
Then, one day, she floored her grandmother by asking,
"Which Virgin was the mother of Jesus ? The
virgin Mary or the King James Virgin ?"
A Sunday school class was studying the Ten Commandments.
They were ready to discuss the last one.
The teacher asked if anyone could tell her what it was.

Susie raised her hand, stood tall, and quoted,
"Thou shall not take the covers off the neighbor's wife."

## Being a Grandparent...

1. She was in the bathroom, putting on her makeup,
under the watchful eyes of her young
granddaughter, as she'd done many times before.
After she applied her lipstick and
started to leave, the little one said, 'But Gramma,
you forgot to kiss the toilet paper
good-bye!.' I will probably never put lipstick on
again without thinking about kissing the
toilet paper good-bye.

2. My young grandson called the other day to wish
me Happy Birthday. He asked me how
old I was, and I told him, '62.' He was quiet for
a moment, and then he asked, 'Did you
start at 1?'

3. After putting her grandchildren to bed, a
grandmother changed into old slacks and a
droopy blouse and proceeded to wash her hair.
As she heard the children getting more
and more rambunctious, her patience grew thin.
Finally, she threw a towel around her
head and stormed into their room, putting them
back to bed with stern warnings. As she
left the room, she heard the three-year-old say
with a trembling voice, 'Who was That?'

4. A grandmother was telling her little granddaughter
what her own childhood was like:
'We used to skate outside on a pond. I had a
swing made from a tire; it hung from a
tree in our front yard. We rode our pony. We

picked wild raspberries in the woods.' The
little girl was wide-eyed, taking this all in. At last
she said, 'I sure wish I 'd gotten to know
you sooner!'

5. My grandson was visiting one day when he
asked, 'Grandma, do you know how you
and God are alike?' I mentally polished my
halo and I said, 'No, how are we alike?''
You're both old,' he replied.

6. A little girl was diligently pounding away on
her grandfather's word processor. She told
him she was writing a story. 'What's it about?' he
asked. 'I don't know,' she replied. 'I can't read.'

7. I didn't know if my granddaughter had learned
her colors yet, so I decided to test her. I
would point out something and ask what color
it was. She would tell me and was always
correct. It was fun for me, so I continued. At
last she headed for the door, saying,
'Grandma, I think you should try to figure
out some of these yourself!'

8. When my grandson Billy and I entered our
vacation cabin, we kept the lights off until we
were inside to keep from attracting pesky insects.
Still, a few fireflies followed us in.
Noticing them before I did, Billy whispered, 'It's
no use Grandpa. Now the mosquitoes
are coming after us with flashlights.'

9. When my grandson asked me how old I was, I
teasingly replied, 'I'm not sure.' 'Look in
your underwear, Grandpa,' he advised. 'Mine says I'm four to six.'

10. A second grader came home from school and said to her grandmother, 'Grandma, guess what? We learned how to make babies today.' The grandmother, more than a little surprised, tried to keep her cool. 'That's interesting,' she said, 'how do you make babies? "It's simple,' replied the girl. 'You just change 'y' to 'i' and add 'es'.'

11. Children's Logic: 'Give me a sentence about a public servant,' said a teacher. The small boy wrote: 'The fireman came down the ladder pregnant.' The teacher took the lad aside to correct him. 'Don't you know what pregnant means?' she asked. 'Sure,' said the young boy confidently. 'It means carrying a child.'

12. A nursery school teacher was delivering a station wagon full of kids home one day when a fire truck zoomed past. Sitting in the front seat of the truck was a Dalmatian dog. The children started discussing the dog's duties. 'They use him to keep crowds back,' said one child. 'No,' said another, 'He's just for good luck.' A third child brought the argument to a close. 'They use the dogs,' she said firmly, 'to find the fire hydrants.'

What is a Grandparent?
(Taken from papers written by a class of 8-year-olds)

Grandparents are a lady and a man who have no little children of their own. They like other people's.

A grandfather is a man and a grandmother is a lady!

Grandparents don't have to do anything except be there when we come to see them. They are so old they shouldn't play hard or run. It is good if they drive us to the shops and give us money.

When they take us for walks, they slow down past things like pretty leaves and caterpillars. They show us and talk to us about the colors of the flowers and also why we shouldn't step on 'cracks.'

They don't say, 'Hurry up.'

Usually grandmothers are fat but not too fat to tie your shoes.

They wear glasses and funny underwear.

They can take their teeth and gums out.

Grandparents don't have to be smart. They have to answer questions like 'Why isn't God married?' and 'How come dogs chase cats?'

When they read to us, they don't skip. They don't mind if we ask for the same story over again.

Everybody should try to have a grandmother, especially if you don't have television because they are the only grownups who like to spend time with us.

They know we should have snack time before bed time, and they say prayers with us and kiss us even when we've acted bad.

A 6-year old was asked where his Grandma lived. "Oh," he said, "She lives at the airport and when we want her, we just go get her. Then when we're done having her visit we take her back to the airport."

Grandpa is the smartest man on Earth! He teaches me good things, but I don't get to see him enough to get as smart as him!

It's funny when they bend over; you hear gas leaks, and they blame their dog.

The other day I went up to a local Christian bookstore and saw a "Honk if you Love Jesus" bumper sticker. I was feeling particularly sassy that day because I had just come from a thrilling choir performance, followed by a thunderous prayer meeting, so I bought the sticker and put in on my bumper. I was stopped at a red light at a busy intersection, just lost in thought about the Lord and how good He is, and I didn't notice that the light had changed. It is a good thing someone else loves Jesus because if he hadn't honked, I'd never have noticed. I found that LOTS of people love Jesus. Why, while I was sitting there, the guy behind started honking like crazy, and when he leaned out of his window and screamed, "for the love of God, GO! Go!" What an exuberant cheerleader he was for Jesus. Everyone started honking! I just leaned out of my window and started waving and smiling at all these loving people. I even honked my horn a few times to share in the love. There must have been a man from Florida back there because I heard him yelling something about a sunny beach... I saw another guy waving in a funny way with only his middle finger stuck up in the air. When I asked my teenage grandson in the back seat what that meant, he said that it was probably a Hawaiian good luck sign or something. Well, I've never met anyone from Hawaii, so I leaned out the window and gave him the good luck sign back. My grandson burst out laughing, why even he was enjoying this religious experience. A couple of the people were so caught up in the job of the moment that they got out of their cars and started walking towards me. I be they wanted to pray or ask what church I attended, but this is when I noticed the light had changed. So, I waved to all my sisters and brothers, grinning, and drove on through the intersection. I noticed I was the only car that got through the intersection before the light changed again and I felt kind of sad that I had to leave them after all the love we had shared, so I slowed the car down, leaned out of the window and gave them all the Hawaiian good luck sign one last time as I drove away.

We could all use a little more calmness in our lives. By following the simple advice I heard on the Dr. Phil show, I have finally found inner peace. Dr. Phil proclaimed, "The way to achieve inner peace is to finish all the things you've started and never finished." So, I looked around my house to see all the things I started and hadn't finished, and before leaving the house this morning, I finished off a bottle of Merlot, a bottle of White Zinfandel, a bottle of Southern Comfort, a bottle of Kahlua, a package of Oreos, the remainder of my old Prozac prescription, the rest of the cheesecake, some Doritos and a box of chocolates. You have no idea how freaking good I feel.

Church Bullentins

These sentences actually appeared in church bulletins or were announced in church services:
The Fasting & Prayer Conference includes meals.
The sermon this morning: 'Jesus Walks on the Water.' The sermon tonight: 'Searching for Jesus'
Ladies, don't forget the rummage sale. It's a chance to get rid of those things not worth keeping around the house. Bring your husbands.
The peacemaking meeting scheduled for today has been canceled due to a conflict.
Don't let worry kill you off – let the Church help.
Miss Charlene Mason sang 'I will not pass this way, again,' giving obvious pleasure to the congregation.
For those of you who have children and don't know it, we have a nursery downstairs.
The Rector will preach his farewell message after which the choir will sing: 'Break Forth Into Joy.'
Irving Benson and Jessie Carter were married on October 24 in the church. So ends a friendship that began in their school days.
At the evening service tonight, the sermon topic will be 'What is Hell?' come early and listen to our choir practice.

Please place your donation in the envelope along with the deceased person you want remembered.

The church will host an evening of find dining, super entertainment and gracious hostility.

Potluck supper Sunday at 5 pm – prayer and medication to follow.

The ladies of the Church have cast off clothing of every kind. They may be seen in the basement on Friday afternoon.

This evening at 7 pm there will be hymn singing in the park across from the Church. Bring a blanket and come prepared to sin.

Ladies Bible Study will be held Thursday morning at 10 am. All ladies are invited to lunch in the Fellowship Hall after the B. S. is done.

The pastor would appreciate it if the ladies of the congregation would lend him their electric girdles for the pancake breakfast next Sunday.

Low Self-Esteem Group will meet Thursday at 7 pm. Pleas use the back door.

The eight-graders will be presenting Shakespeare's Hamlet in the Church basement Friday at 7 pm. The congregation is invited to attend this tragedy.

Weight Watchers will meet at 7 pm at the First Presbyterian Church. Please use large double door at the side entrance.

The Associate Minister unveiled the church's new tithing campaign slogan last Sunday: 'I Upped My Pledge – Up Yours!

To be posted very low on the refrigerator...

Dear Dogs and Cats,

The dishes with the paw print are yours and contain your food. The other dishes are mine and contain my food. Please note, placing a paw print in the middle of my plate and food does not stake a claim for it becoming your food and dish, nor do I find that aesthetically pleasing in the slightest.

The stairway was not designed by NASCAR and is not a racetrack. Beating me to the bottom is not the object. Tripping me doesn't helps because I fall faster than you can run.

I cannot buy anything bigger than a king sized bed. I am very sorry about this. Do not think I will continue sleeping on the couch to ensure your comfort. Dogs and cats can actually curl up in a ball when they sleep. It is not necessary to sleep perpendicular to each other stretched out to the fullest extent possible. I also know that sticking tails straight out and having tongues hanging out the other end to maximize space is nothing but sarcasm.

For the last time, there is not a secret exit from the bathroom. If by some miracle I beat you there and manage to get the door shut, it is not necessary to claw, whine, meow, bark, try to turn the knob or get your paw under the edge and try to pull the door open. I must exit through the same door I entered. Also, I have been using the bathroom for years---canine or feline attendance is not required.

The proper order is kiss me, then go smell the other dog or cat's butts. I cannot stress this enough!

To pacify you, my dear pets, I have posted the following message on our front door:

To All Non-Pet Owners Who Visit & Like to Complain about Our Dogs

1. They live here. You don't.
2. If you don't want their hair on your clothes, stay off the furniture. That's why they call if "fur"niture.
3. I like my pets a lot better than I like most people.
4. To you, they're animals. To me, they're my adopted son/ daughter who are short, hairy, walks on all fours and doesn't speak clearly.


Remember...
Dogs are better than kids because they:
1. Eat less
2. Don't ask for money all the time
3. Are easier to train
4. Normally come when called
5. Never ask to drive the car
6. Don't hang out with drug-using friends
7. Don't smoke or drink
8. Don't want to wear your clothes

9.  Don't need a gazillion dollars for college, and…
10. If they get pregnant, you can sell their children

## Shoebox Dolls

A man and woman had been married for more than 60 years. They had shared everything. They had talked about everything. They had kept no secrets from each other except that the little old woman had a shoebox in the top of her closet that she had cautioned her husband never to open or ask her about..

For all of these years, he had never thought about the box, but one day the little old woman got very sick and the doctor said she would not recover.

In trying to sort out their affairs, the little old man took down the shoebox and took it to his wife's bedside.

She agreed that it was time that he should know what was in the box. When he opened it, he found two crocheted dolls and a stack of money totalling $25,000. He asked her about the contents.

"When we were to be married," she said, "my grandmother told me the secret of a happy marriage was to never argue. She told me that if I ever got angry with you, I should just keep quiet and crochet a doll."

The little old man was so moved; he had to fight back tears. Only two precious dolls were in the box. She had only been angry with him two times in all those years of living and loving. He almost burst with happiness. "Honey," he said, "that explains the doll, but what about all of this money? Where did it come from?"

"Oh," she said, "that's the money I made from selling the dolls."

## IRS Audit

The IRS decides to audit Grandpa, and summons him to the IRS office. The IRS auditor was not surprised when Grandpa showed up with his attorney. The auditor said, 'Well, sir, you have an extravagant lifestyle and no full time employment, which you explain by saying that you win money gambling. I'm not sure the IRS finds that believable.' I'm a great gambler, and I can prove it,' says Grandpa. 'How about a demonstration?' The auditor thinks for a moment and said, "Okay. Go ahead." Grandpa says, "I'll bet a thousand dollars that I can bite my own eye.' The auditor thinks a moment and says, 'It's a bet.' Grandpa removes his glass eye and bites it. The auditor's jaw drops. Grandpa says, "Now, I'll bet you two thousand dollars that I can bite my other eye." Now the auditor can tell Grandpa isn't blind, so he takes the bet. Grandpa removes his dentures and bites his good eye. The stunned auditor now realizes he has wagered and lost three grand, with Grandpa's attorney as a witness. He starts to get nervous. 'Want to go double or nothing?' Grandpa asks 'I'll bet you six thousand dollars that I can stand on one side of your desk, and pee into that wastebasket on the other side, and never get a drop anywhere in between.' The auditor, twice burned, is cautious now, but he looks carefully and decides there's no way this old guy could possible manage that stunt, so he agrees again. Grandpa stands beside the desk and unzips his pants, but although he strains mightily, he can't make the stream reach the wastebasket on the other side, so he pretty much urinates all over the auditor's desk. The auditor leaps with joy, realizing that he has just turned a major loss into a huge win. But Grandpa's own attorney moans and puts his head in his hands. 'Are you okay?' the auditor asks. 'Not really," says the attorney. "This morning, when Grandpa told me he'd been summoned for an audit, he bet me twenty-five thousand dollars that he could come in here and pee all over your desk and that you'd be happy about it!' MORAL?: Don't Mess with Old People!!